No part of this publication may be reproduced, stored in a retrieval system, or transmitted in any form or by any means, electronic, mechanical, photocopying, recording, scanning, or otherwise, without the prior written permission of the publisher, except in the case of brief quotations within critical reviews and otherwise as permitted by copyright law.

NOTE: This is a work of fiction. Names, characters, places, and incidents are a product of the author's imagination. Any resemblance to real life is purely coincidental. All characters in this story are 18 or older.

Copyright © 2022, Willow Winters Publishing. All rights reserved.

Declan
&
Braelynn

Willow Winters
Wall street journal & usa today bestselling author

From USA Today and Wall Street Journal best-selling romance author, W Winters, comes a provocative tale of a club designed for wealthy sinners. It's a story crafted for those of us who crave the villain.

Declan Cross is powerful, brooding, and his dark eyes speak of damage that my soul begs to soothe. I've always been drawn to men who are rough around the edges, the bad guys, so to speak ... but he's a kind of brutal that scares me. So I promised myself I'd stay away. I swore up and down I would never give in to the fantasies that haunt me at night.

One night changed everything. He knows I saw something I shouldn't have. I could plead for my life, but there are no deals or negotiations with men like him.

He made it known in no uncertain terms what he desired most ... And now I'm his.

I'll Kiss You Twice is book two in the Shame on You series. *Tease Me Once* must be read first.

I'll Kiss You Twice

Prologue

Declan

My oldest brother told me once there was a moment when he realized he'd ruined it all. Not just for himself, but for everyone he loved. Carter said it was like time had slowed down, yet it played before his eyes too fast to stop it just the same. He saw everything that would happen — the devastation, the pain, the brutality that lay ahead. And it was all too late. He'd damned us all leading us down a path with no return.

Whiskey slurred his words that night as he leaned against the stained glass window of the church. I vaguely remember carefully taking the nearly empty bottle from him and wishing Jase would drive faster so I wouldn't have to be alone with my eldest brother. He was drunk and nearly belligerent until he spiraled, and that night was hell incarnate for us. The blood that drenched his clothes substantiated that claim. I was only seventeen at the time. Half terrified of what had happened, but more afraid of what my brother would do next.

I remember thinking, never in my life would I allow myself to get to that point. A decade would prove me wrong.

With the motel room's sole small window wide open and the only woman I've ever wanted staring back at me, that moment Carter described comes back to me with a lifetime of pain and realization.

Braelynn is crouched in the windowsill, looking small and weak, in a nightgown far too thin for the cold evening air. The red, white, and blue lights from the streets several floors down below flash across her face. Only moments ago, I held her in the bed that now stands between us. I was going to make things right, but it's far too late. I didn't see this coming. With everything that happened, I could have never imagined this. All I want is to take it all back.

Braelynn's deep brown eyes are reddened, her cheeks tearstained, and the breeze blows wisps of her curly dark hair around her shoulders ... all I can think is at least Carter knew the hell that waited for us. He knew the moment he'd gone too far. I didn't.

The only thing I know as truth now is that everything's my fault and it's all too late.

Pleas for her to not jump ring out through the air as the

metal cuffs dig into my wrists, pinned behind my back. Two men grab me to keep me from running to her, one with the barrel of a gun pressed to the temple of my head as the scream tears up my throat. Pain and adrenaline are nothing when she looks at me like that. Like she's saying goodbye.

She trembles on the ledge and I can't do a damn thing but shout for her to stop. With the police surrounding us in the cramped room and the ending to our story so close, I know she loves me. Her dark eyes hold obvious pain and misery, coupled with so much regret, but more than anything I know she looks back at me, her grip slipping, because she loves me.

She has no idea how much I love her, though.

Or how much this moment kills a part of me I thought was dead until she came back into my life. Something I thought was snuffed out long ago.

Her lips barely move as she whispers to me and a gunshot blasts through the moment.

"Braelynn, no!"

Chapter 1

Declan

Three Weeks Prior

Everything feels colder the moment the doors close at the far end of the hall. They shut with a gentle thud and lock with a soft click, ending my sight of her limp body being carried away. The next steps are simple enough. It's been done a hundred times or more. It's what has to happen. She'll be tortured until the information we seek is provided and verified. And then she'll be dealt with and disposed of. I swallow thickly at the thought.

Her screaming my name in fear is engraved on my heart. Even now in the silence I can still hear it. Dread flows like a fog through me. There have been countless times when I've watched men and women alike struggle against their inevitable fate for daring to go against my brothers and me.

Braelynn, though ... the betrayal runs deep in my veins and chills me to my core.

I can't fucking believe she did it.

"Don't leave her side." I'm only aware I've murmured the command when Nate looks back at me with a questioning look in his eye.

"Boss?" he asks for clarification.

Turning away from the hall they dragged her down, I straighten my shoulders and make damn sure he hears me. "I want to hear her confess."

At the last word, something breaks inside of me. Some childlike hope that Braelynn truly wanted me is irrevocably damaged. She didn't have to love me. She didn't have to care for me in any way. I know that's an impossible task given the man I am. But I thought she craved my touch for the sake of it. I would have happily swallowed a lie if it meant never being confronted with this. She could have wanted me solely for what I can give her—the protection I could have offered her, my wealth—and I would have gladly made a deal with the devil to keep her.

I thought there was something special between us that others could never feel or imagine. A connection that even as a child I knew existed for us and us alone. I'm a fucking fool.

"I want her to tell me, face-to-face before she dies, that she leaked information. That she was working with the feds or, at the very least, Scarlet. I want her to admit she used me. I want to hear it for my fucking self. You won't let her come close to breaking without me there. Is that understood?"

"Boss, I don't—"

"Did you not fucking hear me?" The scream rips up my throat, a heat and adrenaline fueled by anger causing Nate to take a step back instinctively.

The brick walls of the narrow hall make my voice ricochet as I suddenly feel light-headed.

"I hear you, Boss. I'll stay by her side and I'll make certain you are the last one to speak to her."

"If she's not fucking alive, I will kill you myself, Nate." The venom in my words is palpable.

"Yes, Boss."

"I mean it. You stay by her, you watch them."

"Watch them?"

"Make sure they don't take it too far." Even the thought of them hurting her makes me sick. It has to be done. I know it, and yet, every part of me screams not to allow it.

Blood drains from his face. "Is that too fucking difficult? Do I need to do it myself?" I question, my voice hard and my knuckles white from the skin stretched tight as I ball my hands into fists.

"No, Boss. I'll take care of it," he says, the words rushing out of him like he can't say them fast enough.

"She betrayed me in a way no one ever has," I confess to

him against my best judgment. Conflicting emotions swarm through me as I accept the reality. "I will be the last person she sees before she dies. Do you understand me?"

"Yes," he answers weakly and then nods. His gaze drops and the nervousness falls from him in waves.

"You should go, then; don't want to keep them waiting."

I stand perfectly still, unable to move until the doors shut behind me. I've never felt so alone and so devoid of emotion.

The need for revenge, the desire to fight, the anger at being betrayed ... it's all lacking. There's a hollowness in my chest and in the quiet, it feels like an agony I've never known. The back of my eyes itch and as tears brim, I punch the brick wall, over and over. Refusing to believe that she got to me. Refusing to believe I will cry for her. A woman who used me and betrayed me and my family.

What's worse is that they know. I can't hide her from them. They know what she's done. They know what she did to me.

Every muscle in my body screams as my fists slam against the bricks. Getting it all out of me until my bones crunch leaves me how I should be, empty once again.

Chapter 2

Braelynn

Waking up to an ice bath surrounding my lower half, I'm convinced I'm still sleeping even though I'm shaking. I'm convinced the restraints keeping my limbs in place and the thin bars of my iron cage are nothing but a nightmare.

My teeth chatter and it's the only thing I can hear as I slowly come to.

As my heavy eyes open and shivers run up my body, I do everything I can to move away from the cold, to rip myself free. My heart should be racing but it's struggling to get going. As if it's in denial or perhaps unable to run. It's trapped like me. The sound of noisy grinding behind me widens my eyes even further. As my body is lowered deeper into the ice bath, to my waist this time, it's far too apparent this is my reality.

Shock is brutal, but then again, so are the memories as they filter back to me in a blur.

"Help!" I shriek out, thinking I'm very much alone. My voice echoes as my dress soaks up the water, lifting the iced water to my spine. The chill is unlike anything I've ever felt. It seeps into the very depths of my bones.

I've never experienced such debilitating cold before. In a panic, I search the room.

Concrete walls without a single window in sight give the space an oppressive feeling. I'm trapped in an iron cage centered within a large steel tub that's maybe ten by four feet, one that looks aged. Apart from the machine behind me that lifts and drops the contraption I'm in, there isn't a sound in the room to suggest anyone else is here.

The machine groans and rumbles again, the telltale eerie whine indicating movement is imminent and my heart spasms, fearing I'll be dropped farther. "Please help me!" I scream and my words are nearly cut off by the shock of my chilled skin hitting the air.

Thankfully, my body is lifted out of the tub almost entirely, although my ass and the bottom of my feet are still submerged.

Confusion wraps itself around me. I can barely think, waking up from a fog of bewilderment to the shock of the ice bath. All I know is that I'm truly terrified.

"Help me!" My teeth chatter and my shoulders beg me

to hunch over, to collapse my body upon itself and try to get warm, but I can't move. I'm trapped. "Please, somebody!" I cry out, and tears prick as the fear of dying consumes me. The words echo in the empty room and the realization sets in: I'm going to die here.

My lungs still from the freezing cold as the grinding gears signal movement once again. "Declan!" I cry out his name, tears streaming down my face as the glacial sensation travels past where I've been submerged and up to my shoulders, making them convulse.

"He's not coming, Braelynn," a deep, masculine voice from behind me says far too calmly. Shock, and yet somehow hope, beg me to find the source of the voice. I do my best to look behind me, but I can't turn with the restraints at my neck, keeping me bound to the cage. Immobilizing me. The memory returns as clear as if it were happening right now in front of me. Nate killed Scarlet. I turned and he knew I saw.

My heart drops and races at once, and a sickness comes over me. "Declan," I cry out again in a sob. He has to come. He has to know I won't tell anyone.

"I didn't see anything," I murmur although I wish it was louder, "I swear if anyone asks—" I'm trying. I'm trying to be heard, but there's a ringing in my ears and I don't know if they can hear me.

It's silent as I'm lowered farther and I scream until the mechanism stops abruptly. Tears stream freely. I'm fucking terrified.

"You need to tell me who you ratted to and what information you gave them," he says, cutting me off as the cage is lowered deeper into the water. Only a few inches, but still I scream from the spikes of pain that shoot through my chilled body. My toes are already numb.

"Please stop! Declan!" I can't help but cry out for him. He has to know I would never tell. I wouldn't ever rat.

"It will all stop when you give us a name."

A name? What name? I wish I had a name to give. One that would stop this.

"Whatever you think I did, I swear I didn't do it." I can barely get the words out. My body struggles against the bindings, ripping at my skin that's already numb with a tingling pain.

"Help me!" I cry out again as tears stream down my face. With the scream leaving me, I can barely breathe in.

"Just one name, Braelynn, and I'll stop all of this." I don't know the man behind me. I don't recognize his voice, but I swear I hear someone else. Or maybe something else; I'm light-headed from both the fear and the cold. The tears haven't stopped either, nor the trembling of my entire body.

"I sw-swear," I say and swallow thickly, "I didn't tell anyone anything."

With that the grinding behind me begins again as I'm lowered quickly down, and I scream.

CHAPTER 3

DECLAN

The chill of dread overwhelms me with each hard step of my oxfords slapping against the floor carrying a sense of finality as I make my way down the corridor to where they're keeping her. It's as if I'm suffocating even though my lungs are filled with oxygen.

Swallowing thickly, I read the text again. She hasn't admitted a thing and he's unsure of how much more they should push her. He requested they go easy but according to him, it's proving more difficult to retrieve information without pressure. There's a dull thud in my chest at the thought and a sickening churn in my gut.

I won't fucking allow it.

My pace quickens and my numb body moves of its own

accord. There isn't a possibility that the information came from anyone else. I created the false figures in the dummy file myself and my family knows it. It was a test I didn't think was needed, but Carter insisted, and she failed.

She played me for a fool.

As I look around, I hate every inch of this fucking place.

Over the last year, I've spent more time in this wing of our home than my own. Each of us has our own part of the estate, designed for comfort and with anything our hearts desire ... and then we have this hall. I spend my time at The Club or here ... rarely ever in my own corridor anymore.

With my blunt nails digging into my palm, I resist the disappointment that comes over me. I couldn't last five minutes alone in that office, not knowing what Braelynn was saying and how she was reacting.

Carter said I shouldn't watch. He said to stay away until it's done. In this life, you don't disobey. I can't fucking stand it, though. She's *mine*, even if she was only using me.

My throat goes dry and my stomach twists into an iron knot. I can't not watch. I can't stay away. Even if she did betray me, I'm the one who let her in.

My little pet, and her sins, are my responsibility.

Just outside the soundproofed room, I pause, unsure of myself and unsure of everything. Gripping the handle, a single thought pushes me forward: I don't want this dragged out. It needs to be over with. One way or the other.

The dark enclosed space is ten by twelve by twelve feet. It's large enough to house the machinery and equipment necessary for interrogations. The vision of her, behind this door, sickens me. My wish was that she would own up to her deceit, they would leave her for me and then I would see to her end. As much as I loathe it, we cannot have rats among us. And a rat can't leave after witnessing what happened with Scarlet.

But almost two hours in, she hasn't admitted anything. She hasn't said a word and Nate attributes it to going easy on her. All I want is for this to be handled and done. I can't fucking breathe waiting for the end.

Agony seeps into my veins as I open the door and I'm greeted with her screams. Their backs are to me to my left where they watch Ronnie raise the machine. I can't see her from behind it all, but her frantic screams paralyze me with a terror I've never known.

"Just one name and you can come out," Ronnie says calmly with authority, and the anger that rings through me is unnatural and uncontrollable.

"Declan," she whimpers.

"Declan's not coming. Now give us the name of the person who came to you for information."

"Please," she barely gets out, her voice so small and the chatter of her teeth louder than the words she can manage. Every step I take is without my conscious consent. My feet move one after the other. I can feel Nate's and Hale's eyes on me as they watch, dutifully.

"It can all be over for you," Ronnie says. My heart beats in time with every stride until she comes into view.

The sight of her destroys me. *My Braelynn.*

Soaking wet from the top of her head, her dark hair is stuck to the sides of her face, and her eyes are reddened even though her lips are blue. "Declan," she whispers and everything in my vision turns red as her eyes roll back. The iron cage is lowered and she screams out our safe word.

Red. She cries out for me to stop it all.

Out of everything to come from her, out of every word to hear.

My intention was to confront her, to tell her I know the leak could only be her. That I'm the one who set up the trap to expose the rat and that it kills me she betrayed me. I would have given her anything. I was fucking falling for her like a fool.

I saw her interrogation play out in my mind's eye and I hated it, but this... this is a hell I didn't know could exist. "Get her out." I order the command beneath my breath. There's scurrying from behind me, but it's then that she sees me. She's lowered into the water, trapped in a cage and sinking.

Her black dress clings to her and when she sees me, her mouth opens to say something but water rushes in. She nearly chokes on it.

"Get her out!" I scream with a fury I didn't know was possible. The crane grinds and groans as Braelynn sputters.

"Going easy on her." I mutter the words from Nate's text as rage consumes me. They're torturing her. Her entire body shakes as she heaves in air and the cage rises.

"Red!" she screams in a shrill voice searching for me in the dark room, but I've already moved behind her.

Without a thought at all, with everything blurring around me, silently I remove my gun from its holster. I'm only vaguely aware of my actions.

"Boss?" Ronnie questions with thinly veiled fear and surprise before I pull the trigger. The gunshot is muffled from my silencer and practically drowned out by the objections from Nate and Hale. A perfect red circle forms in the middle of Ronnie's head, and the look of shock on his face is almost comical before his dead body falls to the ground, blood spilling from the wound.

"Get her the fuck out!" I scream, not stopping, not waiting, but getting in the damn tub myself.

All I can see is red as I open the locks to the cage. Red blood, reddened eyes, everything is red. Nothing could ever be black and white when there's so much red.

Nate and Hale are quick to act, silently aiding me with no further objections or questions. Hale's shorter than the two of us, a stocky guy who doesn't mind cleaning up messes. But I swear he pissed himself. I can fucking smell it through the faded blue jeans before I spot a stain on the denim.

There's not much focus on him, though, not with her

there, barely coherent.

She's limp and her entire body trembles. Her breathing is labored by the time her body's removed. Deep gouges are evident around her wrists and ankles from her attempts to pull away.

"Declan," she barely manages, her head falling into the crook of my neck. Soaking wet, heavier from the water, and trembling from the cold, I don't think twice about getting her out and saving her. She's unconscious by the time I've pulled her from the cage.

As I climb out of the tub, Nate offers a hand to help me and with Braelynn braced on my left side, I land a punch to his jaw, quick and hard.

He's damn lucky I didn't have the gun in my hand still.

The only thing that saves Nate is the fact that he grabs some towels and a thick blanket. "We tried, Boss," Hale tells me, his eyes wide and the uncertainty and confusion evident. "We added ice but she—"

"I told you not to—" I start but can't finish. Nate stares back at me, hunched over with his hand on his jaw and just as shocked as Hale is. With water seeping into my shirt, I hold Braelynn close to me as I realize what I've done.

"I'm sorry, Boss, I—" Nate starts and stares back at me, "I don't ..."

They were just doing their job. Reality sinks in. They were doing what they were fucking told. I glance at Ronnie, dead on the floor, his wide eyes still open as he lies there.

"Clean him up."

"Yes, Boss," they answer in unison.

My heart hammers hard as I hold her in my arms.

What the fuck just happened? What the hell have I done?

Chapter 4

Declan

Everything is a blur.

With adrenaline surging and a mix of emotions that floods through my conscious decisions, I'm barely aware of anything other than her shivering, soaking wet body that clings to me. The only constant is the soft whimper that spills from her chilled lips down the crook of my neck, like one of a wounded animal, as we enter the kitchen.

We're no longer in the business wing of the estate. The massive space is shared among the family and my brothers' voices echo out as we cross the threshold. The rough laughter of siblings fucking around, joking without a single worry, is instantly iced over upon my entry.

"What the fuck?" Jase's murmur to my left is almost

drowned out by the sound of the chair grinding against the walnut floors.

"What's going on?" Daniel questions from the opposite side of the island where Carter, Jase and Daniel all watch.

Carter, my oldest brother, is quiet but his lethal gaze bores into me.

"She's freezing," I start, becoming more and more annoyed every second they're just standing there. I can barely contain myself and they were laughing. "Help me!" I command and they stare back at me in shock.

Anger brims as her body shudders against me.

Her eyes dart around with fear as she catches sight of them behind me.

"Help me," I whisper, pulling at the straps of her black dress. "I need a blanket," I add, speaking louder, clearer. And to my left, no one moves.

They all stare, bewildered, only watching.

"Get me a fucking blanket!" I scream, the command ripping its way up my hoarse throat.

All the expensive granite and shiny steel of the black and white modern kitchen can't help her. *Why did I come here? Why, of all places, did I come to where I knew they were, when they're the reason this happened?*

Daniel moves instantly, nearly knocking over Jase. Him leaving to help, him reacting eases a fraction of the panic. Only a fraction, though, and her head lolls to one side, unable to remain upright.

"She needs something hot." Jase's words are almost unheard as he moves to the pantry. The cabinet opening is louder than his comment.

"Soup," I answer him with my head spinning.

What the fuck have I done? I don't even know. I peel her clothes from her, knowing she'll warm up faster without them.

She's a rat. They know she is. *Why did I come here?*

Swallowing thickly as I rock her gently, I'm acutely aware of the fact that I want to deny it all. It doesn't go unnoticed that Carter is still behind me. As the drenched clothes slap against the floor, Braelynn presses herself against me and at first I think it's to shield herself from them, but as her icy cold body clings to mine and tears leak from the corners of her eyes, I think it's simply an effort to survive.

My own shirt is soaked and I maneuver it off while doing my best to keep her close. She's cradled against me, so small and helpless.

"What happened?" Carter asks, his voice eerily calm. My throat is dry, my words ragged as I answer him, "It's done with."

"What does that mean?" he questions further, in a tone I can only describe as cautious as Daniel returns with a blanket and holds it out, his gaze nowhere near Braelynn's naked body.

I tuck the blanket around her carefully and as I do, I find myself telling her it's all right. Daniel slowly takes the seat beside us.

"What happened?" he asks.

They all have questions. My heart hammers as I hold her, running my hands back and forth along her skin, rubbing warmth into her. With her hair wet, her lips blue and her unfocused gaze anywhere but on me, I can't fucking take it.

"Declan, what do you mean it's over?" Carter's voice comes out harder this time and Braelynn tenses. She's fucking terrified.

The microwave beeps and Jase is heard scuttering around the kitchen.

"You're going to eat," I tell her softly, ignoring Carter, and brush my nose against her temple to get her attention. Her gaze reaches mine and I'm fucking shattered.

She's not okay. She's never going to be okay after that.

"Declan. What. Happened?" Carter's tone is what snaps the last of my composure.

"Ronnie is dead. That's what!" I scream across the kitchen. Braelynn goes rigid in my arms. "He's dead and she's mine." The finality and viciousness in my words are unexpected. As is the wide-eyed shock that flickers across my eldest brother's face. Jase stands beside him. Both men are powerful, deadly and my elders. Both of them have killed for me. They would die for me.

I can't remember a time in my life when I've seriously fought with any of them. All my life they've protected me. I've never once thought of going against them. Fuck, I only live to protect them and what we have together. I'd be dead if they weren't here. I know it. And yet, in this moment, I hate them.

"Carter," Daniel says from beside me, attempting to ease the tension, just as Jase sets a bowl down in front of Braelynn, who hasn't loosened her grip on me in the least. The silver spoon slides along the rim of the bowl and the faint sound is all that can be heard in the kitchen as my brothers stare at me. Waiting and watching. I ignore them and turn my attention to her.

"Eat, Braelynn," I command her, but she doesn't move, other than the trembling. She doesn't even look at me.

"Declan," Carter starts and Daniel tries to appease him. "Maybe now isn't—" Daniel says, but it's to no avail.

With Daniel seated beside me expressing concern for her and Jase standing behind me with a different concern altogether, Carter looks between the three of us.

All I can do is bring my focus back to her.

She's so small and vulnerable. Her hair still soaking wet, her body still shaking.

I'm on edge and feel everything slipping. "Eat," I tell her, a hardness coming over me as she stares at Carter rather than at me. Gripping her chin, I force her gaze to mine. "Eat."

"Did she tell you—" Carter starts again and my fist slams against the table. The spoon rattles against the porcelain bowl and Daniel leans back. Braelynn's nails dig into my skin as she struggles to hide under the blanket, making herself even smaller than she already is.

"Leave it, Carter," I tell him, my jaw tense, my fist still at the ready.

Daniel stands slowly and with a grip on Jase's elbow, ushers him out.

"We should go," he says loud enough for Carter to hear. His gaze drops from me down to a petrified Braelynn.

I ignore him. He's done far worse than I. If I want her, I will keep her. That is something a man like him should easily understand. It doesn't explain the flurry of agony and loathing that consume me in this moment when I look down and she stares back at him in fear, rather than listening to me.

Just as the thought enters my mind that I don't owe them a fucking explanation, I know I do. I know she's a threat to us all.

"Eat," I command her and she buries her head in the crook of my neck.

I position her how I'd like her, needing her to fucking listen. She needs warmth. With both hands on her hips, not giving a fuck about the blanket, I force her to sit forward. "You will eat, Braelynn," I seethe. The words are spoken from between gritted teeth and with her eyes shut tight, a gasp of a sob leaving her, she reaches for the spoon with shaking hands but she can't grasp it.

I hate them. I hate them all. I hate my fucking life and who I am.

Carter is to my left, still standing in the same place he was when I entered. There wasn't a single attempt from him to help. He says, "Declan, you need—"

Fuck him.

"She's mine!" Lowering my voice and swallowing the lump in my throat, I bring my gaze level with his and tell him, "I will do with her as I see fit."

My tone and words are careful, the threat they contain thinly veiled.

He stares me down for a fraction of a second before finally joining my other brothers to leave. The tension in my shoulders keeps them stiff, until I can no longer hear their footsteps.

I'm left only with a deep wound that's unfamiliar but aches, and a broken Braelynn who doesn't dare look me in the eyes as she cries in my arms.

"Eat," I say, and the single word is softer than before. Gentle and kind, and I hope she hears the remorse I feel. I take the bowl into my own hands and lift a spoonful of the soup to my mouth to blow on it, and to test the temperature before bringing it to her lips.

She's still shivering slightly, but when the first bite is swallowed, her eyes close with a comforting murmur. It's slight, but with tearstained cheeks and color barely suffusing her lips, I'll take the small sign of life from her as a blessing.

The spoon clinks as I dip into the bowl for more warm broth for her.

Whispering gently for her to open her mouth, she obeys and then readjusts in my lap, pulling the blanket tighter around her.

"You're going to eat it all, my little pet. And then I'll decide what to do with you."

Chapter 5

Braelynn

Both the fear and the chill still have a grip on me even an hour after slowly eating soup with Declan warming me. He hasn't let go of me, and I haven't let go of him either but I know it's coming soon. I can't hold on to him forever.

Even though he's taken me through his home, from the vast kitchen and through the den to what he said was his wing and safe, to his bedroom, I barely saw a thing. The terror is blinding and I don't know how I made it out of there alive. I don't know what happened but I would do anything to never go back.

The only image replaying in my head over and over is of the iron cage being lifted and lowered repeatedly into the ice water. I can't breathe, I can't think. All I can do is cling to him even if I can't look him in the eyes.

Did he send me there? Did he know what they were going to do? The questions are so easily answered. I know he did. The knowledge is paralyzing.

"Let go, Braelynn," Declan commands as he lowers me down onto his bed. Still wrapped in the damp blanket, I hold on to it until he tells me otherwise.

"Get under the covers." His tone is subdued, as if he hates this. As if he regrets taking me out of there. He killed him, didn't he? The muffled gunshot comes back to me in a flash. The man who was questioning me—Declan killed him. I know he did. But there were other men present too.

Nate.

Nate was there. My heart races and I try to swallow as Declan takes the blanket his brother gave me. Goosebumps still linger on my skin even though I'm cocooned within the sheets and thick comforter. I'm still freezing, still terrified.

"Declan—" I manage although my voice rasps. Hours of screaming and pleading did nothing but leave what feels like raw and hot deep scars on the inside of my throat.

With his hand on my jaw, he stills me, his eyes piercing into mine. They hold nothing but pain and regret. I can fucking feel it all and I know something has fundamentally shifted between us.

"Hush," he commands me and then leaves my side. Swallowing thickly, I watch his back, the muscles rippling under his damp shirt that clings to him as he locks his bedroom door. My heart hammers in fear.

He told me I should be terrified.

All of the unanswered questions and all my fears rattle through me as I lie helplessly on his bed doing everything I can to have any composure at all.

I'm grateful I can even wiggle my toes. I swear they were blue. The thought of the tub and the ice bath has my eyes shutting tight and my entire body curling up in the fetal position. I'm doing everything I can not to look Declan in the eyes.

Please, let this all be a nightmare. I wish I'd never gone down that hall. I wish I'd never seen Scarlet or what Nate did. I wish I could just go back and wait for Declan like he wanted.

Life is a bitch for one reason only: all our actions are permanent.

As I grip the sheets tighter, I know that everything is wrong and not okay, no matter what Declan whispered on the way down here. When he turns to face me, standing tall and powerful in his suit pants and shirt, he looks so much like his brothers. There's an expression on his face I've never seen before and it warns me to run. That I'm not safe. I was never safe with him.

"I didn't—"

"Don't." He points at me, his jaw clenched and his body powerful. "I don't want to talk about it."

My eyes widen as the shock of his statement warns me from within. I could throw up, with the sudden sickness that churns in my stomach.

"Declan," I manage as I lift myself slightly on the bed, feeling my aching body come back to life.

He cuts me off, though, the weight of reality truly setting in for me.

"I can't hear you lie to me." That's all he offers before he turns from me, pulling his shirt off over his head and dropping it to the floor.

Tears prick and there's a hollowness in my chest. My bottom lip wobbles and pleas beg to spill from me.

"I didn't—" The words come without my consent. Barely voiced as slivers of moonlight filter into the room through the blinds. But he hears me. The man I thought I could love, the man I knew could kill me ... he hears and his answer breaks the last thread holding me together.

"I said hush. The last thing you should do right now is test me."

There isn't a single ounce of warmth left in his words and large, hot tears spill down my cheeks. They soak into his pillow as I lie there numbly, absorbing it all.

I can't help but cry silently. Ever so silently. I don't move, I don't try to wipe the tears away or make a sound at all. I only bury myself in the covers, attempting to survive and live through this. *How?* I don't know how I ever could.

Not when I can barely breathe as it is.

With simple clean lines and varied tones of gray, the

bedroom is just as masculine as it is cold. Each furniture piece is carved from dark, heavy wood. There isn't an ounce of comfort or light. Every detail is consistent and sharp. Even the sheets and comforter on the bed look pristine as if they've never been touched.

The sound of metal clinking is what brings my blurred vision into focus. I quickly wipe at my face when I see Declan staring down at me with a set of cuffs in his hands. My wrists are already sore and have deep cuts in them. His eyes roam down my body and I can practically read his mind. *Pathetic.* I am pathetic and weak, lying ragged in his bed.

"I don't think you need these ..." he murmurs and then drops them to the nightstand with a loud clunk. Before I can respond he says, "You need to sleep. If you kill me, they'll kill you. If you try to leave, they'll kill you. If you lie there as you should, and sleep, you will live."

The weight of his words and the position I find myself in are unlike anything I ever could have prepared for. I almost wish I hadn't fought to live. I almost wish the deadly cold water had just taken me.

I don't ask him if he knew they were going to do that to me. I don't ask him if he told them to do it. I don't ask him anything. I remain silent, closing my eyes and praying that when I wake up it was only a horrid nightmare. Although I am already far too aware that this is my reality. This is what I asked for, loving a Cross brother.

Chapter 6

Declan

With the brutal wind battering the windows in the early morning hours when all the sky is black, I know there isn't a chance in hell I'm going to be able to sleep next to Braelynn. Hours have passed since she silently cried herself to sleep. All the while all I could do was lay here, contemplating the consequences of what I've just done.

I never should have touched her. I knew the moment I saw her that it would be a mistake. Rubbing my hand down my face, I try to rid myself of the image of her staring at me from across the bar, gorgeous and seemingly naïve. Rubbing my eyes harder I wish it would all slow down. I wish I could go back. Regret has never consumed me more.

I'm a fool and she paid the price.

The image of her in the water will be forever engraved in my mind and it haunts me as I lie here. This is all my fault. I've made everything way worse than it ever needed to be.

All because of what? Because she made my dick hard and brought on feelings from far too long ago before I knew shit and still had hope for something else? It was all a mistake.

And now I've fucked us both.

The bed groans as I slowly climb out of it, easing the covers off with care before staring down at her sleeping form. Everything aches with the dread of what's to come. With only pajama bottoms on, I head to the bathroom. Before leaving my bedroom, I quickly slip on an undershirt and grab my phone.

I only hesitate a moment after the door closes with a quiet click. There's no way to lock it from the outside. I settle on a simple truth: if she leaves that bed after I told her not to, she'll seal her own fate. My heart thuds dully as I make my way down the hall. So much is riding on her actions. There's too much I can't control, too many people aware she's been spared, too many eyes watching and waiting.

With exhaustion weighing me down and an unsettling feeling warning me that things have gone too far and the situation's out of my hands, I go to the only place I know is safe.

A bit of hope glimmers when I notice light peeking from under Carter's closed door.

Swallowing thickly, I knock lightly and he must've seen

my approach on the monitor because he calls out for me to come in straightaway.

It's an odd feeling that comes over me as the door creeps open. It's a nostalgia of sorts, like when we first had the estate built over a decade ago. When Carter gave every order and all I had to do was what I was told. When my brothers protected me and I obeyed without question, wanting nothing more than to remain in their shadows. Time has changed everything.

Carter's dark but tired eyes stare back at me, the glow of his laptop screen the only light other than a floor lamp in the far corner. Old books line the left side of his office, while art from Aria covers the right wall in its entirety.

She's changed him in more ways than he knows.

"Can't sleep," I offer and he gestures for me to sit in one of the two leather wingback chairs across from him.

"Same," he answers grimly before closing the laptop. The thick curtains behind him are parted and the moonlight filters in.

As I take the seat opposite him, I remember how he looked at Braelynn from across the kitchen. How he looked at *us*. The regret sours to something else. Something sickening that I can't place. He must read it in my expression because his own changes, reflecting both authority and remorse.

It's quiet far too long, both of us waiting for the other to speak first. His thumb taps against the hard surface of his desk before he takes in a steadying breath.

His lips part but instead of talking, he clears his throat and then glances at the door before looking back to me.

"Tell me what you need," he says, finally breaking the silence. He's wise not to mention her. There's something inside of me that dares him to say her name. That dares him to question me keeping her. Even though I know damn well what I've done is fucked.

I start with the most troubling issue outside of Braelynn and me. "I don't know how to cover what happened to Ronnie."

"Who saw?" Carter questions.

"Nate and Hale." Our conversation is clipped and blunt as I grip the armrests and do everything I can to stay calm and still.

"Nate will understand that you lost it," Carter says easily and then seems to second-guess his wording.

I wave his nervous look off. "I did. I lost control," I admit.

He studies me a fraction of a second before nodding. "Hale was closer to Ronnie, correct? He'll need an explanation. Perhaps Ronnie was given specific instructions that she wasn't—" He sucks in a sharp breath when he realizes he brought her up. "Tell Hale that Ronnie did something which directly contradicted your orders. That is the only explanation that will settle him ... for the moment. Bring him in closer, make sure he knows he's safe and valued, and that you wish you'd told him in advance what you planned to do, since Ronnie had a history of willful disobedience. Unless he's already confided in others. It's been hours. Something like that is hard to keep quiet among men who are loyal to each other."

It's a difficult pill to swallow. Sacrificing good soldiers and then lying to cover up my own mistakes. A numbness comes over me as I nod slowly and respond, "I understand."

"Do what you have to. It's either that or Hale also needs to be silenced."

"Understood," I say and nod, not content with either option but knowing it has to be done. This blood is on my hands. All of this is for her and in direct opposition to how the family operates. Our system only works because we provide for those who work for us. We have control and there are no questions or concerns as a result. We give an order, they comply, and in return they are paid well and their families are protected. It's very simple. Anything unexpected, especially if it can be perceived as a threat, disrupts the delicate balance. Like killing a man who was only doing his job.

That sickening feeling spreads further through me. My gaze falls to the grain in the desk as I wonder what lie would satisfy the fear of being murdered in cold blood.

"It will blow over," Carter reassures me. "They want to believe it will never happen to them. That they are in the inner circle. Tell a lie, no matter how outrageous, and they will cling to it. It being true is the only thing that keeps them feeling safe."

I nod, knowing he's right. "I'll do what needs to be done."

Carter nods once, slowly, but his gaze doesn't leave mine. It's obvious the question is on the tip of his tongue. Cocking a brow I wait, knowing it's unlike him to hold back. But it's also unlike me ... to do any of this shit. I don't create chaos, I fix it.

"What happened tonight?"

A lump forms in my throat as I picture her in the ice bath again, on the verge of death. The moment it all turned red.

"You shouldn't have watched," Carter comments as if he saw it too. As if he read my damn mind.

"I needed to hear her say it," I start, my mind going back to that moment when I heard her scream my name. I'll never know the feel of the ice, but my body goes cold from the thought.

"She will never say it now. Not if you come running to stop interrogations."

"Careful," I warn him, every muscle in my body tensing.

The shock from earlier seems to be lessened, but still my brother's eyes widen slightly. My grip tightens on the chair and I force my back to press into the seat.

"I want to be certain. She did it—there is no way that information reached the feds unless she is the one who gave it to—"

"I know," I say, cutting him off. "I know, but it still doesn't feel right."

"Betrayal never does." He's quick to put forth the advice.

"What are you going to do with her?" he asks and I can't answer. I don't know. All I know is that I don't want her to die. If she's truly an informant, though ...

"What happens when the feds come looking for her?" he says after the moment of quiet and again his thoughts mimic mine.

"I don't want to believe—"

"It's not just you, Declan," he reminds me and there's a plea in his tone. "I understand. More than our brothers, I understand."

Compassion is a rarity from him, and perhaps that's why I confess to him, "I can't kill her until she admits it. I need to hear her say it."

"I'm sure she knows that and she will do anything to stay alive, even if that means lying to you until she can figure out a way to bring you down ... bring *all* of us down."

"How did it get this complicated?"

"You fell for her," he tells me and I hate him for it even if it's the truth. Visions of her flash before my eyes. From when we were children, to when I first saw her glancing at me with those dark, lust-filled eyes, to our first kiss and more. Little moments I've never had with anyone else.

"She is yours, but betraying you is betraying all of us."

"I know," I answer him, pretending as if I'm not completely broken by what she's done. I almost tell him that I just can't believe it. I almost defend her again, but there's no way around it. They all knew I was giving her that file. It was a test and she failed.

For the first time in my life, I wish I had kept some things from my brothers. I wish they didn't know it was her. As I stand up and tell my brother good night, I realize that if I could go back, I'd do it all over again, but I wouldn't tell them about Braelynn. I'd keep it all a secret and keep her to myself.

I can fix this. I can punish her and see to it that she obeys in every way. She has to. There's no other way to protect her and keep her.

"I'll take care of it," I say beneath my breath as I make my way to the door. She's going to regret this, and she's going to make it up to me. She's mine after all.

Chapter 7

Braelynn

It wasn't a nightmare.

The deep cuts at my wrists from where I pulled against the restraints and the pain in my throat of screams that went unheard are proof that it really happened. My entire body is weak, my head faint, and my eyes beg to close and let sleep pull me under again. My racing heart won't allow such a thing, though.

I've barely slept at all and I don't know how I'll ever be able to again.

"You're awake." Declan's deep voice from across the room startles me. With every muscle tense, I stare back at him. Darkness has settled under his eyes, telling me he hasn't slept much either. Maybe not even at all.

"Yes," I answer, not knowing what else to say as I roll over, making the bed groan. It takes a moment to calm even the slightest, but the fear doesn't leave me. Standing there in nothing but pajama pants with his arms crossed, his corded muscles and bare chest are fully on display. Shadows from the early morning twilight play across his chiseled face.

He's always been domineering in his stance and power has always radiated from him, but in this moment he is nothing other than the god who decides my fate. Merciless and hardened by sin, he is the only one who has control over what happens to me. It's never been more obvious and with that knowledge, my throat tightens.

"Your purse and phone are in my office," he says casually after taking a deep breath. His shoulders relax somewhat and he makes his way to me. Each dominating stride is more foreboding than the last.

With every step my heart beats harder, as though banging against the cage of my chest in an effort to escape. I can barely breathe as he kneels on the edge of the bed.

"My mother"—the words rush from me as if begging him for something—"she'll want me to text her." Swallowing thickly, I try to explain as his dark eyes narrow, telling him, "She calls every other day."

Declan's lips pull up into an asymmetric grin as he huffs a humorless laugh. His gaze moves to the right of the room, looking around aimlessly, and I pull the sheets up around me as much as I can. Before I can register what's happening he's on practically on top of me, pinning the covers down and it threatens to expose my chest.

There's nothing between us that can protect me. It's all too obvious as his sharp gaze reaches mine again.

"I can text her for you ... I'm sure that will suffice?" he offers, his tone slightly condescending. Something must have happened as I slept. Something awful.

I remember the last time I told him I was scared, and how he told me I should be terrified. Adrenaline surges through me, but it's no match for how numb my body feels. "Answer me," he commands without an ounce of mercy. Tears prick the back of my eyes as I nod.

"Declan," I say, and his name is a plea that I can't help.

"You're scared?" he says easily, sounding like the devil himself.

I can only nod, my throat closed so tight, I feel as if I'm suffocating.

"Tell me what happened and I can fix this," he offers and it's the first ounce of compassion from him. The tiniest bit but even still, it soothes so much pain. So much fear. My body begs to bow to him, to make myself small and let him comfort me.

"I didn't—"

"Don't tell me what you didn't do. Tell me what happened," he corrects me.

Thump, thump.

"I don't know ... they kept asking me about computer files for your finances ..." I remember the voice, deep and rough without a shred of empathy. I remember the man telling me to just give up a name. I don't have a name. "I don't know." The wretched words slip from me in a whisper as the cage is lowered in my mind and agony betrays any semblance of control I might have.

"Tax evasion and tax fraud ..." he says, coaxing me, climbing on the bed and making his way to me closer and closer, my skin heating with a fire that burns every inch of my skin.

My head shakes on its own as I whisper, "I don't know any of it." The fear climbing by the second, I don't know what to tell him. "I don't—"

"Don't lie to me," he warns and my pulse stutters. I couldn't speak in this moment if I wanted to. Trapped by this man in his room, his rules the only certainty, I've never felt so hopeless and utterly alone.

"Did you ever take the laptop out of the office?"

"No," I answer quickly. I was asked that same thing before in that room. The man asked me that. Flashes crash through my memory. *The ice.*

"When I found you snooping, I should have cut you off then." His brutal tone cuts through me like a knife. "Instead I thought, I'll prove she's isn't out to hurt me," he tells me and his voice cracks ever so slightly. Peeking up into his gaze is painful. Regret and hate stare back at me. "Then you go and fall right into my trap," he continues.

"Stop—Declan, stop please—I didn't—"

"You did," he insists and my entire body goes cold. It feels like being back in that cage. My blunt nails dig into my skin in a desperate attempt to hold on to anything at all.

"I didn't," I plead with him as tears slip down my cheeks. He doesn't believe me. How could he not believe me? "I didn't," I try to speak, but I don't know if the words even come out. So much fear consumes me at this moment that I'm light-headed.

Help me.

He creeps closer, the bed dipping as he does. "Just tell me the truth and I will figure it all out, Braelynn," he nearly whispers.

I don't know what to say, or if I'm even capable of speaking as the events of yesterday play back, faster and faster. Declan says something, but I can't make it out. There's only the iron cage, the freezing water. I can't hear anything as it all whirls by. So quickly all I can hear is the memory of my own screams.

"Tell me," he nearly yells as I see Nate murder Scarlet.

My hand whips out in front of me. I don't mean it to. He's just so close and I'm so scared. My palm burns as the slap rings out and breaks the visions, bringing me right back to the here and now. Shock overwhelms me.

My eyes widen as I realize the fear I felt before is nothing compared to this new terror. Slowly, ever so slowly, Declan turns his head to face me, the red handprint on his cheek evidence of what I've done.

CHAPTER 8

DECLAN

I let her scramble to get off the bed. I let her fall to the floor as she pleads with me for mercy. I let her scurry under the bed, hiding there as I remain perfectly still where I am. I don't allow a muscle to move.

The anger simmers and a sense of failure seeps into me. Failing her, failing us. Everything crumbles when I lose control and I obviously lost it before, but I will not again.

For the sake of her life, I don't allow myself to even breathe as she cries out for me to forgive her, her voice muffled from beneath the bed frame.

My poor little pet.

Every jagged piece of my brokenness feels for her. I remind myself of my conviction, of the only way she makes it out of this alive: *If she gives herself to me, she will be fine. She needs to be mine and then everything will be all right.*

There's not a sound in the dark room apart from her heavy breathing and the pounding of my racing heart. The ability to keep calm and levelheaded has never been more difficult.

"Please don't hurt me," she murmurs in a strangled way.

With every ounce of self-control I possess, I carefully remove myself from the bed. I'm sure to step toward the opposite side of where she is so shifting my weight doesn't harm her, and to give her some distance between us. With slow, deliberate movements, I walk to the other side of the room, press my back against the wall and carefully lower myself to the floor.

Cross-legged and with my head resting against the wall, I let my gaze fall to the shadowy space where she's concealed.

"How did you get yourself under there, my little pet?" I question loud enough for her to hear me. Exhaustion wars inside of me with every mixed emotion I feel.

Failure rings the loudest in my mind. Failing my brothers, failing her just the same.

All because I lost control. I was too weak to take care of her myself.

"I'm sorry," she manages to say but doesn't answer my question. She's resisting my authority and untrusting. She's terrified.

That's how I told her to feel, isn't it? Yet again, more

evidence that I caused this. It was all in my control and then I gave it away. That won't happen again.

I flex my jaw to dampen the sting from her slap.

With both hands resting on my knees, palms up, I tell her calmly, "Come here, Braelynn."

Every second she hesitates anger stirs within until disappointment eventually settles through me. I have to remind myself she's scared because of me. I did this to her. The only one I have to be angry toward is my fucked-up self.

"Come here, be a good girl for me," I calmly command her, keeping my voice even and with a soothing edge. Time ticks by slowly with her mounting defiance.

Her sniffling is heard from the right side of the king-sized bed. "Please don't make me wait any longer, my little pet. My patience isn't what it typically is ..." I swallow down every emotion elicited as the past forty-eight hours flick through my mind. "I've barely slept and I know you haven't either."

The floor creaks as she carefully starts to emerge from under the bed. Her large dark eyes peer up at me and the look in them wrecks me. Genuine fear and genuine sorrow leave no room for anything else.

Her lips are parted as she takes in short inhales, her shoulders shaking with each one.

I watch as the cords in her throat tighten and she swallows, just at the end of the bed, almost out from under it. Her breasts are covered by her long curly hair, tangled from sleep. Even in this moment, with everything that's happened, my cock hardens and aches for her as her naked body crawls to me.

"That's my good girl," I murmur, focusing on her gaze. "Come here," I add and pat my thigh before arranging my hand like before, in a way designed to make her feel safe.

She doesn't make me wait long before pausing in front of me.

"In my lap," I command her and she does as she's told, fitting herself between my still-crossed legs, submissive to an extreme degree. Her breathing is anything but calm, and now that she's in my lap, she struggles to look at me. She doesn't lean against me and her gaze is glassy.

"I'm sorry," she whispers and her voice hitches at the end. As she covers her mouth, I think to keep from losing it, I readjust, rocking my hips to tilt her into my chest, bringing my arms around her to comfort her. Her breasts press against my chest and I hold her there, running my hand up and down her back in soothing strokes.

Her relief is instant as she collapses against me, clinging to me like she did hours ago. I might be bad for her, I might terrify her, but I'm the only escape she has. She will learn that it is enough. I will be enough for her. "Shhh," I hush her, resting my chin on her head as she leans her cheek against my shoulder. With a kiss to her temple, I hush her again.

It doesn't take as long as I think it will to calm her.

"I'm sorry," she says again, her body relaxing more with every passing minute.

"What is your safe word?"

She stills when I ask her, but she answers just the same, "Red."

"I want you to use it more often ... when conversations become difficult. Whenever you feel overwhelmed or in danger. At any point. It isn't just for sex, you know this. You should have used it a moment ago. You know that, don't you?"

She nods into my chest, but I pull her away to look her in the eyes, gently but with a firm hand. Staring into her deep brown gaze, I wait for her to truly look at me. "Tell me you understand."

"I do," she whispers and for the first time, there's a flicker between us. Something raw and undeniable.

"Give me your hand," I order, holding out my own. I don't break eye contact and although her lush lips part and her chest rises and falls faster, she brings her left hand up and places it into mine.

"No, the one you struck me with."

Her body tenses in my hold, but she does as I command. Slowly she maneuvers in my lap to place her right hand into mine. Our locked gaze never breaks, not even as I bring her fingers to my lips and kiss the tip of each one.

With her hand held in mine, I murmur, "You know you need to be punished, don't you?"

She swallows thickly and I swear I can hear her heart racing even as my own quickens. "Yes," she replies, barely getting out the word.

"If you ever did that in front of them ..."

"I wouldn't," she says as if it's a promise, the words tumbling out as she shakes her head refuting the claim.

"I think you would, Braelynn." I'm quick to correct myself, adding, "I know you would. You've forgotten who owns you."

With wide eyes she peers up at me. The look there is one I fucking love, one I would kill for to ensure it stays with her forevermore. Her expression is one of obedience, tinged with the desire to please me, to prove to me that she belongs to me. A warmth flows through me, one that satisfies every jagged edge of what's happened. A balm that promises everything will be all right so long as she listens to me and so long as I teach her, punish her, and satisfy my little fuck toy.

"Yes, Declan," she answers and with that I place her hand on my lap and bring my thumb to her lip.

Yesterday I would have thought it an impossibility to want her like I do now. To crave her begging for forgiveness and promising me her complete submission.

"Who owns you, Braelynn?"

"You do," she answers immediately.

"Do you still want me?" I question and she tells me, "Yes, but I'm scared ..."

"Of my brothers?"

"Yes," she whispers but there's a moment of hesitation.

"Of me?" I surmise.

She nods first before replying, "Yes."

"But you still want me?"

"Yes … I do. Even if I'm terrified of you, I still do," she confesses and emotion drenches every word.

There's a twisted sickness that stirs in my chest, an agonizing truth I've always known was there. I settle on another truth, brushing my thumb along her chin as I stare at her lips. "I can live with that."

"Do …" she starts to question and my gaze is brought back to hers. She searches my expression for something before asking, "Do you still want me?" Her voice is small and full of insecurity.

I'm going to fuck that question out of existence.

If I didn't want her, she'd be dead. I'm certain she knows it, so I bite the comment back.

Instead, with both hands on her hip, I roll her over and then pull her onto her knees. She yelps in surprise, then gasps as I wrap her hair around my wrist and grip the nape of her neck, pulling her head toward me. With her back arched and my lips at her shoulder I whisper against her skin. "There is nothing and no one I want more, Braelynn," I speak without thinking. I tell her what she wants to hear and what I wish wasn't true.

I'm well and truly fucked when it comes to this woman.

"After I punish you, I'm going to fuck you until we're both too exhausted to stay awake any longer."

I keep my grip tight as I lower her cheek to the floor. "Stay," I command her, fueled by her heavy pants. "I want your arms like this for your punishment," I tell her and lay them beside her, palms up so she can't brace herself any longer. My gaze lingers on a gouge on her wrist from where the restraints dug in.

Betrayal and anger, disappointment and even fear strike me. For a fraction of a second, they all war inside of me. Every emotion demands to be heard and I smother them all down, refusing to feel anything but what I have with Braelynn in this moment.

Running my hand down her back, inwardly I promise myself I will make this all right. Her shoulders carry the weight of her upper half, her ass remaining high in the air and her cunt barely showing to me.

"Arch your back," I murmur as I stand behind her to take off my pants. My erection is hard and eager for her, but my palm itches to punish her first.

She does as commanded and I'm given a perfect view of the soft hues of her pink lips. Getting back down on my knees I grip her hips and drag her away from the wall to position her so I have full leverage behind her.

She yelps with the movement and nearly moves her arms. They jerk from natural instinct, but she keeps them how I arranged them.

Good girl.

That's my good little fuck toy.

I don't give a shit what happened before, I'll keep her away from everything and she'll stay safe and she'll stay mine. That's the only thing I care about.

"Safe word, Braelynn. Give it to me."

"Red," she whispers, a flush already darkening her tan skin. The color pools in her cheeks as she breathes in heavily, her hands clenching and unclenching as she waits for the first blow.

I grip her ass in my fist, squeezing and tugging slightly to bring her blood to the surface.

"What is your punishment for?" I question her to make damn sure she knows.

"Hitting you," she answers with a pained, hushed tone. Her eyes close tightly and I tell her to look at me. From where she kneels beneath me, naked and bare with her back bowed, her dark eyes peeking through her thick lashes, I've never wanted anything more. Her submission is perfect. She is all that is beautiful between us, all of what is worth fighting for.

As I squeeze her ass again, bringing a hint more pain, her bottom lip drops slightly and a crease forms between her brows. "You'll never lay a hand on me again. You'll never yell at me again. If ever you feel the need, you will safe word, I will take care of you and we will continue when we are ready. Do you understand?"

I already know I never want to have this discussion again. She isn't going to tell me who she leaked information to. She'll take it to her grave. So long as she obeys from here on out ... I can live with that.

"Yes, Declan," she answers dutifully and I waste no time running the tips of my fingers up her slit and then down to her nub. She's not wet enough yet, not ready for me, but she will be when I'm done with her punishment. Her body will beg me for my cock.

The first smack is light and her arms jerk slightly beside her, but she remains still. I waste no time giving her a second smack, this time using the back of my hand on the other side on her ass. Not hard, just enough to pinken the skin, to prepare for what's to come.

Grabbing her ass where I've just spanked her, I press my cock into her thigh and lean forward to scrape my teeth along her neck. I nip the lobe of her ear once and then whisper to her, "It is done, it is taken care of, do you understand? This is the end of it."

My heart batters inside of me as her eyes widen and she stares ahead blankly. Her expression is pained. She desperately needs me to believe her ... but I don't. I can't. I can love her, though. I can protect her. I can make sure she's never in this position again. We just need to get through this moment.

"Yes, Declan," she answers and I kiss her fiercely. Her gasp is short and her moan much longer as I taste her, as I rock into her. With one hand on her breast, I squeeze and she moans lower and deeper. I reward her by plucking her nipple and she shivers against me. My smile breaks the kiss and she's left breathless, staring up at me with questions coloring her beautiful gaze.

"Your punishment first," I remind both of us and get in position behind her.

I need her ass bruised so even after the high of her orgasm is long gone, she remembers this punishment. With that thought in mind, I strike her right ass cheek with a swift blow. Her instinct to move gets the best of her and her arms come up, her palms on the floor as her mouth drops with a silent scream. My left hand grips the nape of her neck and I hold her down.

"Count them, my disobedient pet," I command her as my pulse quickens and my heart pounds. She's slow but deliberate in placing her arms back down at her sides, palms up like before. "One," she barely gets out. My mark on her is bright red and I'm certain stings worse than my palm does. When my hand comes down for the second blow, just beneath the first, tears leak from the corners of her eyes but still she manages, "Two."

Releasing her neck, I use my left hand for the other side.
Three. Four.

Tears fall freely as I rub her ass, squeezing and kneading her flesh.

"You're my good girl now, aren't you?" I question her as I play with her cunt.

"Yes, Declan," she grits out in a pained voice. Lowering my lips to her clit I suck before taking a languid lick up her slit and dipping my tongue in her hole. With a hand on each ass cheek I squeeze, teasing out the pain I'm giving her as I suck on her clit once again.

A deep groan of satisfaction leaves me as her pussy clenches around nothing, arousal sweeping away any lingering discomfort.

Kneeling behind her, my cock juts out and I run a hand up and down her back, soothing her as I tell her, "You have ten. Six more to go."

Her expression stiffens as does her entire being, but she answers how she should. "Yes, Declan."

"You're the perfect little fuck toy, aren't you?" I question her and just as she answers yes, my palm strikes down.

Her breathing hitches with obvious pain, but she counts like a good girl.

"You'll never disappoint me like that again, will you?"

Her voice is tight as she answers no at the same time as my other palm comes down. I'm careful to check where I've struck her, and monitor every inch of her.

Just as I'm about to tsk, she whispers, "Six."

"Good girl," I murmur as I rub her cunt and she's so desperate for relief, she rocks into my hand.

"Greedy little slut, aren't you?" I question, staring down at her. She's fucking gorgeous, her eyes closed and her lips parted just slightly.

"For you," she answers and that's when I know we're going to be just fine. I can keep her safe and I can keep her mine. I keep reassuring myself, I keep telling myself that everything will be perfect and as it should be as I spank her ass and upper thighs until she's sobbing. Every inch where I've struck her will be bruised tomorrow. My own hand stings and is practically numb from the blows.

Smack!

She's mine. They will never touch her again. She will never betray me again. She's mine.

Smack!

"Ten," she cries out on the last one louder than the others. Her shoulders heave as she does, her chest rising and falling chaotically.

She winces as I grip her ass with both hands, squeezing again. She may be in pain, but the moment I thrust into her slick cunt, all the way to the hilt in a swift motion, utter rapture takes over her expression.

Buried inside of her, I move her arms up, letting her brace herself with her palms on the floor. "You're going to need to hold yourself up," I tell her as I pull out slowly.

She whimpers with the loss, her head hanging to the side.

The moment she looks back and her eyes find mine, I slam inside of her. The sight is a fucking drug. Like heroin to my veins. Her tearstained cheeks, her parted plump lips and her dark eyes beg me to fuck every thought of what's happened out of her pretty little mind.

I rut into her savagely and without warning, needing her to come on my cock. Her nails dig into the carpet as she's pushed forward. I'm all too aware that with every thrust, she has both the pain of her spanked ass and the pleasure of me fucking her heightened.

Kissing her wildly, I capture her stifled moans with everything in me, needing her to feel overwhelming pleasure. With her lips on mine, she comes undone beneath me, her body tensing and her pussy clenching around my cock.

I resist every urge to come and ride through her orgasm, fucking her harder and deeper, taking her to the highest high imaginable.

I fuck her ruthlessly until she's limp beneath me, barely cognizant with my name spilling from her lips as if I'm her fucking savior.

Chapter 9

Braelynn

The first thing I note when I wake up is that Declan isn't in bed. The second is that every inch of me is in agony.

My throat is on fire, my muscles are sore and tight, and my ass is in such pain that I wake from rolling over onto my side.

Fuuuuuuuck. Gritting my teeth, I absorb the shock of the sudden pain. With a deep breath it's gone in an exhale. I slept like death itself. Pure exhaustion that still lays heavy under my eyes left me without a single dream or nightmare.

Yesterday comes back to me all at once. Shivers run down my spine and I cling to the blanket. Everything is okay, I remind myself even though it hurts to swallow, my throat is so hoarse. I remember screaming his name last night as he fucked me like I was his whore. I wish I hadn't. It already hurt before and now simply swallowing brings about pain.

Add in a headache that's more than likely from lack of caffeine and waking up is a new kind of hell.

Vaguely I remember the balm Declan rubbed on my backside last night. Retreating to my stomach, I lift myself up enough to check his nightside table. A white jar and a tube of Neosporin sit next to a large black glass clock. It looks just as heavy as it does expensive. Everything in his room does. That clock, though, is something else.

It could either kill you, or make you go broke to own it. The thought brings a touch of humor to a rather uncomfortable morning. I'm quiet for a moment, listening for Declan. I watch the bathroom door, but it's shut and there's not a sound in the room in the least. The bed groans as I make my way to the nightstand.

Every muscle in me aches, even muscles I didn't know I had.

The memories of last night come back to me as I gently rub the cooling balm over my heated skin.

My heart flicks with a painful beat as I remember him whispering in the crook of my neck that he loved me. *I swear it happened, didn't it?*

He carried me from the floor to the bed, although I don't remember it. My gaze drops to my knees which bear evidence of carpet burn. He fucked me into a rag doll last night. The memory of how savagely he took me steals my breath and hardens my nipples. The ache between my thighs outweighs the soreness of any other part of me.

I don't know if it's the lack of sleep or the hell of what's happened, but I don't remember it all. It's in pieces. All I know is that he said it was over, he said he wants me, he said I am his and no one will ever touch me again.

And I promised him obedience and submission. I promised to be his. Something tells me there is fine print to this unwritten contract that I'm not prepared for.

Heat consumes me and I do my best to ignore it as I take care of myself, every so often glancing up and expecting him to be standing in the doorway.

He never appears, though.

It takes me a good ten minutes before the balm goes into effect enough for me to scoot off the bed. The soreness is much more manageable on my feet although I'm freezing without the covers.

Still naked, I venture to the en suite bathroom. There, a toothbrush and hairbrush wait for me on the edge of the counter. They're both pink and still in packaging.

After calling out his name and even peeking beyond his bedroom door to the vacant hall lined with a textured dark blue wallpaper, I determine he's left me alone.

Every dark mahogany drawer begs me to open it, but I resist. I go about my business in the bathroom, carefully placing the items back where they were and the packaging into the trash.

It's only when I come out of the bathroom, feeling somewhat better after drinking water from the tap that I see the shirt laid out on the bench at the foot of the bed with a note.

It's written on a thick piece of parchment.

I won't be gone long. If you wake up and need me, call me from the phone in the kitchen.

Feel free to make yourself more comfortable. Do not leave the wing unless it's to go to the kitchen.

He's left only a simple Henley for me to wear. It's his and quite large so the hem of it rests around my upper thigh. I can't lie, a single sniff of the shirt reminds me of him and it soothes the pain of not knowing what's going to happen for just a moment. It vanishes quickly as the headache reminds me of its presence.

I reread the word *kitchen* and debate on waiting for Declan before leaving. The attempt to sit on the edge of the bed proves to be painful so I'm quick to get back to my feet. With the note in my hand, I take in my surroundings. It's all heavy foreboding furniture, no pictures or knickknacks. Everything looks expensive and cold. There's not an ounce of personality and nothing sitting out to occupy my curiosity.

There isn't a television either. There's nothing but quiet.

A chill runs over my shoulders and I debate on opening a

drawer in search of pants or socks even, but I don't.

If he wanted me to wear something else, he'd have given it to me. His comment about me snooping also comes to mind and a freezing cold grips my shoulders. I glance at the note again and then the bedroom door. I debate on lying down again, on simply sleeping—as if I could without remembering what happened before last night—until he's back. I nearly do it, too, but a spike of pain rips through my head.

Caffeine withdrawal and starvation are a bitch.

Unable to fight those off any longer and the continued quiet leading me to have thoughts I would rather not deal with, I decide the kitchen is where I should go. Declan might even be there waiting for me.

Maybe that's why he wrote it in the note.

An eerie feeling clings to me as I open the door and look out into the hall again. "Declan?" No one answers me. It's so quiet I can hear my heart racing.

The kitchen led to a large foyer, and that foyer opened onto Declan's wing ... I'm almost certain. My heart beats harder, but I'm almost positive it was that easy. If it wasn't, surely he wouldn't have allowed it.

I shut the door behind me, the note he left still in my hand and I cross my arms over my chest as I wander down the hall.

The dark navy blue color palette is a constant down the long winding hallway. The doors are carved dark mahogany, and every one of them is shut. There are three doors in total that I pass. Two on the left and only one on the right before coming to the double doors that exit to the foyer.

I debate on knocking on them, on testing to see if Declan is there but then I read the note again.

My palm is damp as I hold the parchment tighter.

Whatever I do today, I can't disappoint him. Not again. Fear still lingers and there's a dread that doesn't let go of me.

I'm not given much time to think on it as I step out into the massive foyer. The black and white marble tiles feel cool against the soles of my feet. Heavy walnut double doors with carved crystal doorknobs lead to what I know to be the other wings of the estate. I know there are five in total, one for each of the Cross brothers, and the last ...

My gut roils at the thought of where that fifth door leads and I hurriedly avert my gaze. Swallowing thickly, I continue straight ahead, my bare feet padding silently on the marble flooring.

This home is unlike anything I've ever seen. It's more of a mansion than a house. I've heard rumors and stories about this place, but nothing could have done it justice.

Light pours in from the massive windows in the sleek, modern kitchen. Just beyond the back wall that's lined with black glass from floor to ceiling, I think I can see a garden outside. It's so much brighter here compared to the hall where there wasn't a single window, or to his room where all the curtains were pulled tight.

The entire kitchen is spotless as if it's just been cleaned and smells of a hint of lemon. The dark walnut floors are polished to such a high shine, I can see my reflection in them.

I only get two steps into the kitchen, without an idea of where the coffee machine would even be, when I hear the distinct sound of masculine voices behind me. Their heavy footsteps are sudden and their tones casual.

With my heart racing, I spin on my heel with fear striking through me at the sight of the Cross brothers.

Silence slips between us as the three of them walk in, then immediately halt when they see me.

All three are dressed for the day. Jase and Daniel wear slacks with a button-down and polo, respectively. Carter is in a slim-fitted, dark gray suit with no tie. They could tell me the cufflinks Carter wears cost more than my mother's house and I would believe them. From the way they've all styled their hair, to the clean shave of their sharp jawlines, wealth drips from them. So does their savagery.

And then there's me, surprised and underdressed, alone and in the middle of their kitchen where I know I don't belong.

In only the Henley that Declan left for me, I cross my arms over my chest in an attempt to hide myself. The motion breaks up the three of them staring. Jase and Daniel avert their gazes to exchange glances.

Carter doesn't look away, though.

"I was just—" I start to explain as my pulse pounds

in my ears, fear churning in my gut, but the pain hits me unexpectedly and my hand comes up to my throat.

"You all right?" Daniel questions and I remember last night when he brought me a blanket, before Declan told me all of this was over, sealing that deal with a rough fuck and I was able to get a few hours of sleep. Without my consent, my gaze moves to the table and I wish the blanket was still there so I could cover myself with it.

"Do you need help?" Jase asks when I don't respond.

"Just ..." I try to answer, but with the three of them there, assuming or thinking things that aren't true, and Declan nowhere to be found ... a dread cold creeps inside of me and all I can think of was what happened the last time the three of us were here.

"It's okay, just ... what is it that you need?" Jase presses, snapping me out of it as he approaches me, brow raised along with his hands. He looks me in the eye. "Did Declan give you any ... instructions?"

I don't know why the truth keeps me silent like it does. I've always known they kill people. Even if I hadn't seen it, I've known since I was a little girl that these men are bad. Being alone with them after what happened yesterday is more than a little overwhelming and my words fail me. A wave of lightheadedness comes over me and I nearly feel faint until the sound of a chair dragging across the floor grips my attention.

"Sit down," Carter commands from across the kitchen,

his hand still gripping the back of the chair.

My body moves on its own, propelled by fear mostly, but I have to be careful as I sit. I suck in air through my teeth and wince, but I take a seat as directed.

Even through the pain and through the pounding headache, my focus remains on the fact that all three of them are watching me. When I look up, Carter stares back with slight concern.

"Do you need an Advil?" Jase's question comes with the shake of a bottle and I watch him as he closes a cabinet.

"Yes, please."

"Let me get you water too," he comments.

I nearly tell him I can do it, wanting to confess I just came in for a cup of coffee and I didn't mean to bother them, but instead of the statement leaving me, the words stay put at the back of my throat. I grip the edge of the table as if it's keeping me grounded. Daniel and Carter are still staring, even though Daniel has the decency to glance away when I look up at him.

Carter doesn't. The only thing that pulls his attention away is his phone pinging in his hand.

Whoever it is, he answers with a text as I accept two white pills and a glass tumbler of water from Jase.

"Coffee?" Daniel questions as I throw the medicine back.

I swallow the pills and water quickly, nearly choking on them to answer, "Yes, please."

As I hand the glass back to Jase, my hand trembles and I

wish I could stop it. I nearly drop it. I wish I could control myself.

"You all right?" Jase asks, eyeing me closely.

"Just a little under the weather, I think," I tell him as a shiver travels down my spine again. "I didn't mean to intrude."

The noise of the coffee grinder roaring to life startles me and the three of them stare at me once again. Heat engulfs my entire body. Flashes of last night come back to me, one by one, as I glance at the chair next to me. The one Declan held me in.

I feel fucking sick. Like I'm about to heave up a mostly empty stomach.

"I'm just glad Declan didn't lock you in a tower somewhere," Daniel comments lightly, as if it's a joke, but I can't manage the energy to even smile at the thought.

"It's a joke. Just thought he might not let us see you again for a while," he explains and Jase elbows him, muttering something into his ear just as the coffee machine that I can't see sputters.

"Do you have a fever?" Carter questions, and I look back up at him. One breath in and one breath out is what it takes to steady myself.

"I'm just cold," I answer him, once again wishing for that blanket. As if reading my mind, Daniel emerges once again with a blanket for me, handing it over while keeping his distance.

It's quiet as I wrap it around myself and I try not to look at them because I feel my throat getting tight and the emotions overwhelming me. All I can hear is the murmur of men and then the clink of a spoon against ceramic before Jase brings me a cup.

"Cream and sugar," he says and I answer, "Yes, please," before looking down.

"He said you liked it that way I mean," Jase explains and that's when I realize he's already added both.

"Declan messaged," Carter states from across the room. He leans against the counter and motions to his phone.

"Oh," is all I can respond as the questions rampage in my mind. *Is he happy with me?* is one of the loudest, followed by, *Am I going to be okay?*

"He said you're allowed out," Carter tells me and I hear him stepping closer so I look up, both of my hands wrapped around the mug. "He also said that I shouldn't be an asshole to you."

Jase and Daniel huff a laugh at his comment and I wish I could too, but I am very much not okay and far too aware of that fact.

With a sweep of pain at my temples, I finally sip the coffee. My eyes close instantly as the warm runs through me and the froth of the coffee is licked from my lips. Like everything else in this place, it's exceptional.

A moment passes and it's fairly quiet apart from Jase

and Daniel discussing something lowly by the fridge. A part of me wishes they would leave, so this panic in me would subside. But another part of me doesn't want to be alone. I just want Declan back. I wish more than anything that he hadn't left me.

It takes another sip of coffee and every ounce of courage I have in me when Jase looks back at me to ask him, "Where's Declan?" I know Carter is still right there, watching me, and I'm also aware it was evident that I asked Jase and not him. A chill sweeps over me, followed by a heated sensation, causing me to shiver involuntarily.

"He had to take care of some things at the office," Carter answers, not Jase, and I'm forced to meet his cold gaze. I don't think the man can help it. He simply elicits fear.

Bringing my attention back down to my coffee I thank him, unable to hold his gaze.

I don't expect Jase to break up the quiet with further explanation. "Because he wants to stay home with you to help you adjust. So he has to wrap some things up first, that's all."

"Adjust? That's what he said?" I can't help but question. There's something soothing about what Jase just told me, something encouraging although I'm all too aware I would cling to any hope at this point.

"Among other things," Jase tells me, nodding and then he leans against the fridge. I catch Daniel smirking next to him before he turns to the pantry.

"Like what? What other things?" The words leave me before I realize I need to shut up in the hopes they'll forget I'm here.

Daniel murmurs what sounds like a scolding that Jase ignores apart from cracking a smile.

"He's happy you're able to walk," Jase tells me and a violent blush overtakes my cheeks.

I pull the blanket tighter around me, wondering what else he told them.

"You're Braelynn with the pigtails?" Daniel questions and Carter answers for me as my heart pounds in my chest. "No."

Pigtails? My mother used to braid my hair in pigtails every day for middle school. Back when I first knew of them. It feels like an eternity ago.

The fridge door closes and Daniel stands there with a stick of butter in one hand and block of cheese in the other. "Yes she is," he confidently corrects Carter, looking at him before meeting my gaze. "You are, right?" he questions me. "From school?"

I can only nod, swallowing down every insecurity. I can't imagine they would remember me at all. They were years older and I only ever shared a couple of classes with Declan. Of all the things to think about right now, the day in gym class in middle school when we were playing jump rope comes to mind.

"Declan had a puppy dog crush on you," Jase comments and I glance up to find him smirking. Daniel grins as he goes about making what looks to be a grilled cheese and then I glance at Carter, who stands in the same place, only now he's openly staring, so hard that I can practically see the wheels spinning.

He's intimidating, the other two much less so.

"You like grilled cheese, right?" Daniel asks.

Although my stomach is empty, I don't have an appetite in the least. I can't imagine saying no, though.

As if he can hear my thoughts, Carter tells me in a more soothing voice, almost hypnotic, "I think it would make Declan happy if you ate."

There's a knowing, a kindness in some way in his tone. Something shifts between us and I answer softly, "I would like that."

Carter only nods once, not moving and then returns to his phone, but as I sweep my gaze to the cooktop, I catch the other two sharing a glance. One that's a balm for the smallest bit of uneasiness in me. One that allows me to sit in the chair, huddled in the blanket and sit with them in relative silence. It's only once Daniel puts the sandwich in front of me that they leave the kitchen and I belatedly realize not a single one of them ate. They didn't get themselves food or even drinks.

I do, though. I finish every bite of grilled cheese and every drop of coffee ... but once I'm back in Declan's room, alone except for the memories of yesterday, it all comes right back up and I'm only grateful I made it to the trash can in time.

Chapter 10

Declan

As quietly as possible, I push the door open. It's only as the door creaks that I glance down and see the blood under my thumbnail.

Shit.

I still for a moment, watching her lie in bed under the covers. Listening for any hints as to whether or not I've woken her up. It's been hours of watching her from my phone, tossing and turning at first before falling asleep.

She needs it, my poor girl.

Satisfied that she's undisturbed, I head to the bathroom first to wash away what I had to do this morning and afternoon. Hale is a risk. One I can't allow to exist. Or "was," rather. He *was* a risk.

He bore the weight of my mistake. It's unfortunate, but so very many truths are.

As I wash my hands at the sink, I swear I can hear him begging me not to kill him over the sound of the running water. He swore he didn't steal from me. And he didn't. I didn't have to believe him, it was everyone else in that room who needed to think he was lying.

It went well enough, with him apologizing and begging. A single plea for forgiveness was enough to condemn him in the eyes of my men.

One man's false confession brought him death. It's an unsettling feeling. And then there's Braelynn and what she went through.

Turning the faucet off, I'm left with the uneasy quiet but not for long.

"Declan?" she calls out, hesitantly.

As I step out into the bedroom, I unbutton my shirt halfway down and then pull it over my head. When the fabric falls, I catch sight of her. A messy halo of hair from sleep, and her eyes more rested, bracing herself on her stomach ... in my bed.

If only she wasn't sick, I'd rid her of that shirt and bring us both the closure we need for this fucked-up week.

"Lie back down," I command her and she does as ordered, her arms under the pillow, elbows bent and her cheek resting against it. Kicking off my pants, I question her, "Carter said you got sick and haven't eaten all day?"

"I did eat," she answers with her wide eyes on mine. "Jase brought me soup a little bit ago." She glances at the bowl on the nightstand, which is empty apart from the lone spoon. I brush the hair from her face with the rough pad of my thumb and Carter's right, she has a fever.

"I was gone longer than I thought I would be," I explain. "I'm sorry I wasn't here to help you." I'm gentle with her, all the while thinking this is yet again my fault.

"I'm okay," she whispers and leans into my touch. *Good girl.*

The bed protests as I climb in and under the sheets to join her.

"Show me your ass, my little pet," I tell her as I pull the comforter back. A dark bruise colors her right cheek and another is on the underside of her left. My cock is instantly hard and all I want in the entire world is to squeeze her ass while playing with her cunt to give her both the pain and pleasure she needs.

She's not well, though, so balm it is.

I take my time, rubbing in the soothing cream. At first she winces, sucking in a breath through her teeth. But then her body melts under my touch, relaxing apart from a chill that runs through her.

"How are you feeling?" I question her.

She shakes her head, her hair falling down her shoulders as she does. She's fucking gorgeous, even unwell. Her tan skin and dark features tempt me as always. "I don't feel sick to my stomach anymore."

"Was it something you ate?" I ask casually although I have an idea what happened. I watched her stare at that chair beside the bed until she threw up.

"I don't think so, just … I just think everything caught up to me maybe," she answers softly, testing each word, careful with it. Her body tenses as if she's afraid of what my reaction may be.

"I don't want you to think about whatever it is that made you feel unwell," I tell her and she stiffens further, her eyes wide open but staring fixedly on the headboard as I close the lid to the balm. She doesn't agree, she doesn't answer me and just as I reach down to bring her attention to me, she speaks.

"It's all I can think about, Declan."

I still, her chin in my hand as she peers up at me.

"I don't know how to not think about it," she says and her bottom lip wobbles slightly. "I don't want to think about it."

"Then think of me. Every time you think of what happened, you give that to me."

My thumb runs along her lower lip. Her skin is hot and flushed from the fever. "You give me that fear and I will take care of it."

"How?" she questions.

I know that I shouldn't. Everything inside of me screams not to say a damn word to her. That she doesn't need to know and that if she does know, if she is lying to me and she's that damn good, I'll be fucked. But when she looks at me like that, I can't help it. I can't let her sit in that kind of pain and agony. "The men who hurt you are dead, Braelynn. No one is ever going to hurt you again. I promise," I tell her and my pulse rages inside of me. I can't guarantee that if she's lying to me. All day today I've gone back and forth with whether or not I can trust her. Either way, though, even if she is a fucking rat, she is mine. And either way, this woman is my downfall.

I can't fucking help myself, though.

She is my mistake to make and I would do it all over again.

"Even Nate?" She whispers the question and I swear I can hear her heart pounding.

"Did Nate hurt you?" An anger barely contained brims, tensing every muscle inside of me.

"No," she says and shakes her head, "he was there when we left."

"He's the one who messaged me," I tell her, carefully, but not giving the exact truth.

She searches my expression for something, I don't know what but it's irrelevant. Gripping her jaw, I tell her, "Look at me. You will give this to me. Any worry, you make sure I know it and I will take care of it. Any thoughts like what happened today, you tell me them and I will take care of it."

"Declan," she whispers like she's scared. Like whatever she's about to say is a secret she's afraid of speaking aloud.

"You can tell me anything," I whisper and my chest

spasms with pain as I will her to confess to me. "Whatever has happened, or will happen, I will take care of it and you. Nothing outside of us matters. You are mine. No matter what ... happened."

"Declan," she murmurs and there's such vulnerability in her eyes. "I didn't do it. Whatever they told you, I didn't do it. I swear. I would never do anything to hurt you."

I hold it together, although something inside of me breaks. I know she's the only source of the leak. I know that as a fact. But I caress her jaw and I kiss her tenderly. With my eyes closed and my lips close to her, I give her another white lie. "I believe you."

I want to believe her. Everything in me *wants* to believe her.

I cannot risk it happening again, though. Everything is in place to ensure she's never given vulnerable information again. With that in mind, I pull back, staring down at her as she peers up at me like I've soothed every concern.

She will not be a liability because she will stay far away from all of that.

"No one will ever touch you again and you have no reason to be worried, my little pet."

She reaches up to kiss me and I meet her lips but keep it short, petting her hair and then kissing her temple. Her skin is blazing hot.

"Now rest," I whisper as I run a soothing hand down her back, then pull the covers over her. "I don't want you sick."

With a sheen of sweat along my forehead, I wake up in a panic, my heart racing, the screams still very easily heard. Every muscle is coiled and it takes me a moment to realize I'm in my bedroom and Braelynn is beside me. The night terror dims until I can barely remember what it was about.

Blinking it all away, I get out of bed and it protests the shifting weight with a groan.

The covers rustle and her soft voice cuts through the quiet night. "You're awake."

With heavy lids and her hair a mess, her bare shoulders peeking out from under the covers, she watches me. Out of instinct, I lean across the bed and cup her cheek in my hand and then test her forehead.

"Your fever hasn't broken yet …" I glance at the clock and then back to her. "It's three fifteen, go back to sleep and get better so I can have you as I wish."

A soft smile graces her lips but it doesn't reach her eyes. "It was hard to sleep. You sounded like you were having a nightmare." I'm caught off guard and don't react at first. "Are you okay?"

"I'm fine," I tell her and perhaps it comes out harder than it should. Regaining my composure, I lean over and pull the covers up around her shoulders. "I didn't mean to wake you, go back to sleep."

She watches me intently, her eyes much more open than before. "Will you be here when I wake up?"

"Do you want me to be?"

"Yes."

"Then I will be."

Just as I'm answering her, shivers run down her shoulders and she holds her pillow tighter. Climbing back into bed, I put off the nightly routine when this shit happens. When I come home and can't sleep, when 3:00 a.m. wakes me with messages of murderers, a bust, someone threatening someone else not paying. All of the bullshit of this fucking business that keeps me up with a strong hand and a hardened heart.

"Come here," I tell her and pull her closer to me, holding her by my side. My brothers said they would take care of it. They told me to wrap up any loose ends and then they would take care of everything else.

My only task left this week is to decide what to do with Braelynn. Her feverish body is burning up as she nuzzles next to me. She's far too warm to be seeking my touch for comfort but she presses against me as if she can't get close enough. She's mostly lying on her belly, but resting some on her side. With my arm around her I hold her close, splaying my hand against her shoulder.

With a single kiss to her temple, I tell her to sleep. I stare at the ceiling and reassure myself again as my thumb rubs soothing circles on her skin. My brothers will take care of work and I will take care of her.

It's a first. They've never had to cover for me since I've stepped up to my current role. In over a decade, it hasn't happened. Not since I was a fucking child. Every goddamn day there's a fire to put out and I question if they're capable of handling things like they used to be before they all settled down or if something will inevitably fall through the cracks.

"Are you sure you're okay?" The softly spoken whisper brings my attention to the woman in my arms. My shoulders rise and fall as I take in a heavy breath.

"Is my fuck toy questioning me?" I smirk down at her and her concerned expression eases. "Does your ass not remember what happens when you push me?" As she blushes and writhes slightly in my grasp from the memory, I kiss her temple again and then nudge her nose with the tip of mine to kiss her lips.

She pulls back ever so slightly before saying, "I don't want to get you sick."

"There you go, taking on burdens again," I murmur and then kiss her lips, taking them with possessiveness. Her lips linger and I deepen it slightly, rewarded with a moan of pleasure from her.

Her hand rests on my chest and with the movement she winces.

A bruised ass, wounds on her wrists and ankles ... and now

she's sick. My poor girl. If I could go back, I'd have lessened the bruising. Perhaps skipped it altogether.

A huff leaves me at the thought. If I could go back, I wouldn't have pushed her to the point of slapping me. Running a hand through my hair, I remind myself, all of the what-ifs and should haves don't mean shit. They're nothing but irrelevant fuckups.

I simply can't do right by her. It's one thing after the other and nothing is right.

"Could you tell me a story?" she questions, once again bringing my focus back to the present.

"You think I know bedtime stories or fairy tales?"

"No, no," she murmurs, "just any story."

"I'm not exactly known for my storytelling skills."

"I can't ... stop thinking," she says quietly into her pillow and doesn't look me in the eyes. "I keep thinking about the ... Scarlet and the bath." Mixed emotions swirl inside of me. The very mention of Scarlet, a known traitor, has me wondering why she's bringing it up. There's no question she was a rat. We had her on camera, recordings from phone calls, her texts and photos of her meetups.

Clearing my throat, I try to think up a story. "You want me to distract you?"

"Yes ... please."

"One time, a long time ago ... there was a kid. He was dirty all the time because he hated showers and his brothers were always gone." I almost add "and his father was always drunk" but I realize it would be far sadder than I want by adding that detail in. We only had one bathroom in our home and the memory of my mother falling in it when she was weak and frail and I couldn't help her haunted me, even after she was gone. I don't tell her that either, though.

Her breathing is steady, her breasts pressed against my chest as she listens to me. "And one day, this little girl who was sweet and so cute, told him he smelled."

She lets out a small laugh and a genuine one, albeit gruff and short, leaves me too. With a small smile she looks up and tells me that's not what she said.

"Might as well have."

"I was polite," she argues in the most adorable tone.

"What was it you said?" I ask her, trying to remember that moment.

"I asked if you needed somewhere to go for a bath."

"Mmm, I don't remember it like that."

"I wanted you to come home with me and I would have helped you. That was before, though," she comments.

"Before what?" I ask without thinking.

"Just before things changed."

I offer her a sad smile. Things changed all the time when I was younger. Every month worse than the last. Lonelier. Harder. I'm not naïve enough to think it wasn't worse for my brothers. I don't remember it all, and my father wasn't as hard on me. He beat the shit out of them, though, and all I did was hide in the corner. Regret makes it hard to swallow as memories I don't care to recall come back.

I remember my mother dying. I was so young I only remember a few things before that. And Braelynn with her perfect braids and frilly dresses telling me I needed a bath was one of them.

"There's a happily ever after, though."

"Is there?"

"The boy made sure he showered every day after that," I state somewhat comically. She doesn't laugh so much as roll her eyes and make an effort at a tiny smile.

"That's the happily ever after?"

"I told you, I'm not the best at stories." The blanket falls from her shoulder as she shifts so I pull it up around her again. "The boy would have done whatever that girl told him to," I tell her and I don't know why. Maybe that sounds like more of a happy ending. It isn't, though, because I hardly saw her again. Let alone spoke to her.

"He didn't tell the girl that," she whispers and then her hand comes up in a balled fist as she coughs.

"He didn't tell anyone very much at all," I say, testing her forehead again. She's burning up.

"Do you want more tea?" I ask her as she rubs her throat. I could get it for her, but I'd rather she sleep, unless it's hurting her and keeping her up.

"Don't leave me," she answers. "Please."

"Awful bossy, my little pet, and that doesn't answer my question." I smooth the hair back from her face as she breathes in easily and shakes her head. "No, thank you."

"Go to sleep or I'll be forced to tell you another horrible story," I tell her half-heartedly joking and she laughs. The sweet sound tugs my lips up into a weak smile.

I lean in for another kiss but she pulls away slightly with a frown. "I really don't want you to get sick."

"If I do, I do," I tell her and kiss her again. "Leave the worrying to me, my little pet." I kiss her once more and when I open my eyes, hers are still closed.

I leave a gentle kiss on her forehead again and whisper, "Sleep well." The heat from her fever lingers as she drifts off. It's worrisome that she's been sick all day and seemingly getting worse.

It's only once she's asleep that I text the doctor and he's quick to reply, asking for her symptoms.

Declan: *She's not hungry, she's tired all day and night. She started coughing today. She's worse than this morning. I think it's only a cold but events occurred and I want to be sure.*

Doc: *Is it possible to bring her in? Or for me to come to her?*

A thought wriggles its way into my mind and I answer him: *We'll come to you.*

Chapter 11

Braelynn

I've never liked hospitals. My mother doesn't like them either. They don't hold good memories and it seems absurd to go see a doctor when all I have is a fever.

The dull white noise of the engine purring and the wheels turning isn't comforting.

A nagging thought won't quit ... one that whispers we aren't going to the hospital. That he doesn't believe me or he doesn't want me. His frustration and distrust seem to come and go. I don't know what they told him, but I can't help but feel like he doesn't believe me.

From the corner of my eye, I watch him as we sit at a red light. As if his expression could tell me anything. I'm a fool to think I know him.

A voice in the back of my head warns that I'm even more of a fool to think he'll keep me safe. Or that he would choose me over his brothers. I have to look away and stare out the window at passing cars to keep my thoughts from becoming obsessive.

When Declan places his hand on my thigh, I nearly jump out of my skin.

"You feeling okay?" he questions, his voice soothing and deep. He's so calming, so caring, I'm suddenly feeling riddled with guilt with where my thoughts have led me.

"Mm-hmm," I answer, pulling the sweater tighter. I hope he can't hear how unsteady I am in my voice. I don't want to be. More than anything, I don't want to feel this way. I'm in borrowed pajamas, albeit extremely nice pajamas and a sweater that probably costs more than my rent.

"We'll be there soon," he tells me and lifts my hand in his so he can kiss each knuckle as he drives. His hand doesn't leave mine as he lowers it back to my lap. My tortured heart can't take it.

Even if I am a fool, I'd let him lie to me right now. I'd happily accept it so I can stop going back and forth, so I can stop thinking about it all like he told me. I wish I could pluck every morbid thought and memory from my mind. It feels as if I'm going crazy in a way. I'm spiraling but desperately trying to hold on to him. As if he can make everything okay when it's so obviously not.

"Are we okay?" The question tumbles out of me and I can't believe it did.

"Of course," he answers and yet again, I'm left wondering if what I'm feeling is all in my head. I am sick. And the fever can't be helping anything.

"Are you scared?" he asks and that alone eases some of the insecurity.

"Yes," I answer.

The atmosphere immediately chills between us, but yet, there's still a spark. "You can safe word if you're scared." He pauses. "Say it."

"Red."

With the click of the turn signal, my heart races as he pulls over to the side of the road. It's not until the car is parked that he speaks again. "You safe word, we pause, I fix whatever is wrong," he says as if it's truly that simple. As if there isn't a problem at all with everything that's going on. His hand grips my chin and he stares deep into my eyes. I wish he wouldn't. I'm worried what he'll find there.

"Why are you scared?" I can barely breathe at the question. It seems in direct opposition to what he told me before.

The truth slips from me anyway. "I feel like … maybe what happened before …" I swallow thickly as his jaw tenses. "I'm afraid I'm going to do something and it's going to happen again because I swear I didn't. I didn't leak anything or give anyone anything or say anything." My voice cracks on the last word and my breathing quickens. "They said I gave information to someone. I didn't, though. I swear I didn't." As the words rush out of me, Declan forces me to look at him, his hand on the back of my neck. His hold is so possessive it silences me.

"The only way anyone will ever touch you again is if you leave me." His expression is nothing but deadly serious with a hardness I've only seen from him a time or two. "Do you understand that?"

"Yes," I say, the single word coming out in a breathy voice, feeling a heat between us that has nothing to do with sickness.

"You stay with me, you do as I say and you are safe. I don't care what anyone else says or what they want, or what they think or what they tell me. Do you hear me? I don't give a fuck. I'll slit their throat before they can say a damn thing to me about you. Do you hear me, Braelynn? You are mine. I choose you."

With a single beat of my heart a second passes before I whisper, "You promise?"

"I don't like that you're questioning it."

I confess, "I don't either."

He leans back in his seat and it groans. His attention turns from me for a moment as quiet settles between us. Twisting his hand around the leather wheel, he looks back at me. "I allowed someone to come between us. I know that I did and I am sorry, Braelynn. I never should have allowed it.

It won't happen again."

My heart thuds in the faintest way. Like it gives in. Like it believes him with its entire existence. I know right then and there, he's ruined me.

"I promise," he adds.

"Thank you," I murmur, caught in the emotion that swirls in his gaze. A million things about this man have me doubting my sanity, but I don't question that he wants to keep me safe and that he has the power to do so.

His tone shifts to one that's more demanding. "I don't want you to think about it anymore. I don't want you to worry anymore. I've made those points clear, haven't I?"

"Yes."

"You are only to worry about pleasing me. That is it. Everything else is mine to take on. Give in to that and you will feel so much better."

His hand grips my chin again and his strength is weakened. "For fuck's sake, Braelynn, you're sick. Don't worry about this. Not now and not ever again. Do you promise me?" he asks, emphasizing the words with his brow cocked.

"I promise," I answer him and he grips my hand like that act puts an end on the conversation.

"You make me a desperate man," he comments and a half smile pulls at my lips. I wonder to myself, at what point did the tides change between us? I start to think as he pulls away from the shoulder and the soft hum of the car soothes my nerves, that maybe this was fate and it was meant to happen. For whatever twisted, fucked-up reason that the universe has in store for us. I start to think that the worst is behind us.

If only that voice in the back of my head would stop whispering that I should be terrified and that it's going to happen again.

It's only a fever, but it still sucks walking into the hospital feeling mostly dead and pathetic. I wish I looked halfway decent, especially compared to Declan, who's got his arm wrapped around me in support. Shamefully, I'm happy to lean on him as we stand at the reception desk. In dark wash jeans and a Henley, no one would know who he is. He still radiates authority, though, and a darkness that's only swept away when he smiles. Which he doesn't do for even a second as we stand there in silence, waiting for one of the two receptionists to look up. The first woman is closest to us and scribbling something in a notepad; the other has her back turned, tapping away on a computer.

Both are in light blue scrubs so I wonder if they're also nurses.

"Checking in with Doctor Jacobson," Declan says evenly and calmly, but with an authority that has the young woman in front of us peeking up from the notepad. Her horn-rimmed glasses are bright teal, her lips the perfect shade of cherry red and her dark hair is pinned back in a high bun on her head. She's young, much younger than the woman behind her who looks over her shoulder the moment the first questions, "Name?"

"Mr. Cross," the older woman with bleach blond hair says and pushes her chair back so quickly it nearly tips over. "I'm sorry for the wait, right this way."

The brunette in a bun seems to realize who he is right before my eyes. At first there's confusion and then we're given wide eyes as the blood drains from her face.

"My apologies; she's new here," the woman leading us attempts to explain before clearing her throat and ushering us to an elevator.

It's quiet as we ride up the elevator, stopping on a floor that requires a code. It's unsettling, and I find the fever competing with an anxiousness that makes me feel sicker than I think I am.

All the while, Declan holds me, comforts me and leads me down a quiet hall, far too quiet and then into a private room.

It's ... jaw dropping. What. The. Fuck.

"I didn't know rooms at the hospital existed like this," I murmur as I stop short of the hospital bed in the middle of the room. The bed itself is adjustable and that sets it apart from a posh hotel room. But the linens are luxurious and the furniture reminds me of the estate.

Expensive, clean and modern.

The nurse opens sliding doors to an armoire and behind it is various equipment.

"Dr. Jacobson instructed me to prep you, if you don't mind." The nurse turns to me. "I'm so sorry, I seem to have forgotten your name," she comments with the same tension she held downstairs.

"Braelynn Lennox."

"It's nice to meet you, Ms. Lennox. I'm Nurse Rachel and I will be here for anything you might need." She stands at attention and then gestures to the bed, "If you don't mind, would you kindly lie down."

Declan leads me to the bed and with the fever, I'd nearly forgotten the bruises on my ass. Wincing as I sit down prompts the nurse to question, "Is it just the fever?"

Fierce blushing colors my face as I glance over at a smirking Declan, even though his eyes still hold a look of concern. He helps me lie down as he tells the nurse my symptoms. Fatigue, loss of appetite, fever and a cough.

It's uncomfortable lying down and I wish I could lie on my stomach, but I can't.

Declan is a silent observer as Nurse Rachel takes my vitals and then hooks me up to the machines, monitoring every possible thing from my heart rate to oxygen levels.

"She's been in pain, can you get her morphine?" he says the moment the nurse informs me that the doctor will be in shortly.

She hesitates for only a second. "Of course. Just one moment, I'll get that right away." Not a question is asked.

"Are you all right?" Declan asks me and as I look up at him, he glances at the monitor and then back down to me.

Nodding, I answer, "As fine as I can be." The nurse returns with two pills and a glass of water. Not a paper cup to throw away, but a heavy glass that looks like carved crystal.

Before I've even thrown back the pills, she asks if we need anything else and Declan answers for me. "That's all, thank you."

With a short nod, she leaves us.

"So ... this room is ... yours?"

"My family's. The hall is ours."

My brow rises in surprise.

"We have our own doctors and staff," he explains. I keep forgetting the rules are different for men like him. Hell, they make their own damn rules — the normal ones for people like me don't apply to the Cross brothers. As if exemplifying my thoughts, Declan places a thin black phone into my hands. It's lightweight and obviously expensive, and definitely not mine.

"What's this?" I question with confusion.

"Your new phone."

"Can I have my own phone back?"

"I'd rather you have this one," he says and shrugs, casually, as if this isn't an invasion of my privacy or an insult or something I should be upset over. My mind races with every possible reason he took my phone. I can't explain why it feels like such a loss. It's only a phone but my photos are on there; I chose that phone. I saved up for it and bought it myself. It's a piece of me. Even though it's only a hunk of metal.

"Declan—" I protest but he doesn't let me finish.

"What did I say about worrying? You give it to me." He answers his own question.

I bite my tongue, not at all content with so much changing so quickly. One thought comes back to me, though, the same as the other day. "I would like to text my mother." We talk often, very often and I'm sure she's messaged. "She'll worry about me."

"Then text her," he states and gestures to the phone in my hand.

"She won't recognize—" He cuts me off before I can get my point across.

"It's the same number ... just a different phone," he explains. "All your contacts and information are there for you. Nothing's been changed or deleted."

"Why did—"

"It's needed, and I don't want to have to explain it to you. I want you to accept what I give you, without hesitation, without concern. It's only a phone, my little pet. There are so many other things you will need to simply accept. Do you understand?"

It's tense between us for only a moment.

"Yes, Declan."

"I will not make changes that aren't necessary," he tells me, standing closer to the bed. He pulls the covers up closer to my chest as he adds, "You know that, don't you?" I nod in agreement with him. When I do, he kisses my temple.

Do I know that, though? I know he spoils me, I know I feel safe with him. I know I love what he does to me and that there's something about him that has always pulled me to him. I know that I don't want to lose him and that a phone isn't worth a fight.

So long as I can talk to my mother.

"Are you monitoring it?" I ask him and he gives me a smile as he replies, "Of course I am."

I swallow thickly and pull slightly away from him.

"It's for your protection," he tells me and the machine monitoring my vitals gives away my anger as my heart beats faster. The bastard beeping earns a glare from me that makes Declan smirk.

"Hey," he says, bringing my attention back to him and I'm met with pleading eyes and a calming voice. "There's no reason to be upset or angry with me. Every one of us has a phone with a tracking and monitoring device in it. When I say it's to protect you, I mean it."

"Okay," I concede, far too tired to argue and acutely aware of the power imbalance between us to think that I have any say at all.

I am his. I suppose it's only just now dawning on me exactly what that entails. One thing that hasn't left me is that I'm scared of him. That fear holds me back more than he knows.

"I'm going to get you some soup from the restaurant next door. My brother said they have the best and he would know, given he's been in this room more times than all of us combined."

"Which brother?"

"Carter." His name stiffens my shoulders. I'm not sure he ever won't intimidate me.

"He likes you. He's ... hard and cold, with no people skills to speak of ... so it might not come through," he tells me with a crooked smile. As if it's a joke. "I know he isn't exactly approachable."

"If you say so," I tell him and a wave of hot and cold come over me. I wish I could break this fever. I don't know if I've ever had a fever for so long. I blame the stress. It's a killer.

"You have your phone ... call me if you need me," he tells me and doesn't move to stand. He stays by me, hovering over me as I lie in the bed, waiting for me to agree. "Understand?"

There is something in his hazel eyes, something that tells me he needs me to give in to him, when he stares down at me. I'm entranced by it as his fingers travel down the side of my neck, his thumb along my throat. It's the gentlest of touches, yet so possessive, so him. "Yes, I understand." He's a powerful man, far stronger than I've ever truly given him credit for. But it's not the physical dominance that eclipses this moment, it's something else entirely.

"Good girl," he whispers and kisses my cheek. My eyes close and I breathe in his scent. When he does that, comforts me and calls me his "good girl," it's like nothing else matters. I've grown far too fond of it, far too ... reliant on it to feel well. The warmth of Declan's touch is gone the moment the room to the private door closes with a resounding click.

Alone in the room, I'm left with the steady beeping from the monitors as my only company and the hope that the pain meds will kick in soon. I stare at the door a moment too long and my thoughts go astray. Back to the unsettling feeling that what happened before will happen again.

That I know better than to be with someone like Declan and my greatest fear now is that it's no longer my choice if I'm with him or not.

With that spike of fear, I consider pulling off the contraptions monitoring my vitals and running. Going anywhere but here. It's all too much and not what I signed up for. My throat goes dry at the thought.

Go where? My inner voice sneers, *They'll find you. They'll kill you and he would never forgive you if they didn't end your life.*

Despite everything that's happened, I trust Declan. More than that, I fucking love a piece of him even if other pieces of him terrify me. But he did say, the only way anyone would ever put their hands on me again is if I left him. As the implications of what that truly means get the better of me, a chill runs through every inch of me right down to my bones. I try turning in the bed as if I can get away from it all, as if I could simply stop the reality from weighing on me like it is.

What the fuck have I done?

My thoughts are interrupted by a knock at the door and my heart races yet again reflecting in the rapid beeps of the monitor. A voice I don't recognize calls out, "Ms. Lennox?"

"Yes. Come in," I answer and attempt to calm myself.

An older man with glasses and white hair, clad in a white lab coat and name tag reading Dr. Jacobson, walks in. His gaze immediately zeroes in on the machine beeping far too quickly. His thin lips press into a firm line and then he gives me a smile when he looks back at me, a clipboard in his hand and a sympathetic look in his eyes. He might not know the details, but I'm certain he knows this room is for the Cross brothers and that there's more than one thing that ails me.

"Let's see how I can help you, Ms. Lennox."

CHAPTER 12

DECLAN

"She's not pregnant, right?" Carter questions as I walk into the small room in the back of the hall. From outside it would seem like a utility closet; in fact, that's what it used to be before we took over this place.

"No, asshole." I answer him firmly but with the same smirk he wears, although, to be fair, it would make everything so much easier if she were. If she was pregnant and we got married, she couldn't testify and she wouldn't want to leave me.

"No judgment," he comments with a smirk.

"They rushed the blood work," I tell him and pass him a stack of papers that all boil down to one simple fact: it's just a cold.

"Not pregnant and everything else is in normal ranges." Guilt still washes over me. The stress and temperature extremes from the bath obviously caused it. She's not well because of them ... because I allowed them to take her. My tone drops as I tell him, "She's sick, but she'll be fine."

I watch her from a few rooms away where the closed-circuit monitors are stationed. The doctor fusses about her, asking her questions while physically examining her. Dread and guilt stir in my chest as she tells him she got locked out of her friend's house in the cold rain a few days ago.

"Want to sit?" Carter asks as he takes a seat himself and I join him, attempting to hide how on edge I am.

The small room is much less comfortable, with only three chairs, a long desk that takes up the length of the room and four monitors that display the camera footage from the exam room.

"Is it recording?" I question.

"We can if you'd like. This is your show," he tells me.

"No need," I answer him, feeling nerves prick the back of my neck as the tension gets the best of me. It's only the two of us; no one else even knows this is happening. Just in case she says or does something she shouldn't.

"So it's just a cold, that's a good thing."

"I would never forgive myself if it had been anything serious," I tell him without thinking much of it as the doctor leaves and she's alone in the room.

"You have strong feelings for her."

"I like her, Carter, I told you that."

His gaze doesn't waver but I turn my attention back to the screen, even though I can feel him willing me to look at him.

"Any idea why she threw up?" he questions and his tone is more ... concerned than expected. It's hard to know what he makes of her. I think whatever happens today will add to his judgment either way.

"She said she was just thinking about what happened. Just a queasy stomach over ... everything that happened." I swallow down the bitter knowledge.

"That's understandable," he comments in a murmur. We've all had our fair share of squeamishness over some of the shit we've done and certain things we've been through.

They've saved my ass more than once but I'll never forget the first time I stared down the barrel of a gun. We were in a shoot-out and cornered in the back of the warehouse we were working out of. By all accounts, we shouldn't have made it out alive. Even the memory of that moment makes my heart race and a cold sweat line the back of my neck. I stared down the gun that was about to end my life and I knew I was going to die.

I didn't see Carter's gun at the back of the guy's head. I watched as he shot him three more times for good measure, though. Standing over him, Carter's expression would have been the definition of a hateful gaze if not for the way he glanced back up at me. His eyes were filled with the fear of loss. He waited for me to stand, to catch my breath before handing me the spare gun in his holster. I wasn't the only one who thought I was going to die right then and there.

"You think she needs help for that?" he asks and my hackles rise.

"Help? Like what?" I bite back, hating how he's battering me with questions and that I don't have a good fucking answer for them. "She's fine," I tell him with finality.

"I don't mean any offense by it ... just that she might want someone to talk to?"

So now instead of wanting her gone, he wants her in a fucking padded room? I keep the snide thought to myself.

"Calm down, Declan," he tells me and his hand lands on my shoulder. "I'm not judging. I'm only trying to look out for the both of you. You want me to shut the fuck up? I will."

My throat tightens as the uneasy emotions wash through me.

"You're scared of what she's going to say?" he asks and gets right to the bottom of it.

"She said she didn't do it, but it's not like the feds could have hacked it."

He watches me as I struggle with the frustration of it all.

"And you're wondering what if she's lying to you?"

"No. I'm wondering what if she really didn't? What if she went through that shit because I didn't give her a chance?" The words escape me with more emotion than I'd like.

"You really think they could have possibly gotten it any other way? You were the one who set it up and for good reason."

"She's not dumb, but she can be naïve and maybe something happened where she didn't mean it and she didn't realize what she was doing."

"The odds of that are slim, Declan."

"I'm aware ... So here we are," I say, then gesture to the monitors and right on cue, Mike and Brian appear on the screen, walking side by side in expensive suits down the hall.

My pulse races. "I fucking hate this."

"The things we do for love," Carter murmurs.

"Whatever happens—"

"She's yours. I won't tell a soul and whatever you'd like to do with her, whether it was an accident, whether she's actively working with them ... whatever you want to do, she is yours for you to deal with." He pats my shoulder once before leaning back in his seat. "I'm only here because you asked me to be."

I face the screen just as they walk in, and rub the back of my neck as if that will keep the nerves from wreaking havoc. "We don't have to do this," Carter reminds me.

"No. She said she didn't do it. If she's working with the feds ... well, then we'll know."

Be my good girl, Braelynn.

I don't know what I'll do if she fails this. I don't know how I'll ever be able to look my eldest brother in the eye again if she takes this bait.

Chapter 13

Braelynn

The moment it seems as if the morphine has kicked in, and all of the pain and soreness vanishes, two men walk into the room unannounced.

No knock, no warning.

I only realize they're cops when the one on the left holds up his badge and tells me he's Detective Barlowe and his partner is Detective Hart. Both of the men are clean-shaven, in sharp suits and with fresh haircuts. The taller one, Hart, seems older; he's a Black man with wrinkles around his eyes and so far, he's been quiet. It's his counterpart, a younger white guy with sharp hazel eyes who's doing all of the talking.

My stupid heart races and the monitor displays that truth all too loudly, with the incessant beeping picking up.

Shit, shit, shit.

"No need to be nervous, Ms. Lennox, we just have some questions for you."

All I can think is: *Fuck. This.* My heart hammers and the beeping continues to reveal my agitated state. Irritation overwhelms me to the point that I want to rip off the pulse oximeters, and it takes everything in me not to. Instead I focus on calming down.

I can handle this. It's going to be okay. Declan is going to be back any moment.

The back of my eyes prick, wondering what Declan will think. Wondering if he'll believe me.

"I'm sick," I tell them bluntly but they don't stop. They both step closer, surrounding me on either side of my bed.

"We heard ... do you have time to answer our questions?" Detective Barlowe asks.

"I'm very tired and I don't think—" I start but again, they don't take the hint.

"We've cleared it with the doctor and this will just take a moment." Detective Hart speaks up for the first time, his voice far more commanding and low, seductive even. He catches me off guard.

Swallowing thickly, I answer, "Just one second, please."

I start to pull the covers down and then ask them for privacy. "Just a moment, please. I'm very hot." Ever the gentlemen, they turn. "Let us know when you're ready."

I fumble with the phone Declan gave me. It's embarrassing how my fingers tremble. With every second, I steady my breathing, I attempt to look anything other than suspicious although I'm certain that's exactly what they think of me.

I send the red flag emoji to Declan. I nearly put the phone down but then I decide to record this bullshit. He's going to know exactly what happened. I hit record and wait a moment.

"You don't need to text your lawyer, Ms. Lennox," Hart jokes when the tapping is more than obvious.

Satisfied that its recording, I lower the phone to my side and place it face down so they won't know and pull off my sweater. "Not my lawyer, Detective," I tell him, forcing the semblance of a smile. "You can turn around now."

"Had to let someone know we were speaking?" Hart questions and Barlowe follows up with, "Would that be Mr. Declan Cross?"

My heart does a skitter of a beat and I clear my throat as the damn monitor gives it away. Both of the men look at it and it pisses me off. *How is this fucking legal?*

"Do my text messages matter with regards to ... whatever you're here for?"

He starts to push me for the name of who I messaged and I cut him off by asking, "What is all of this about?"

I'll be damned if I'm giving them anything.

"What happened to your wrists?" Hart asks in a tone that's much more concerned than prying. I can feel the blood drain from my face. I swallow thickly, staring at him as I think of an answer and do everything I can not to think of the water. The cage. The voices I can't see. The fucking cold that I thought would kill me.

"Self-induced?" Barlowe presses when I don't answer.

"If you must know, bondage is an especially favorite kink of mine," my smart ass answers.

All of the pent-up anger and frustration spews out of me with disdain. The cops honestly don't deserve this venom. They're only doing their job and they didn't do a damn thing to me. I could be polite or even silent. Instead, I don't hold back. I'm all too aware it's because I'm so damn careful with Declan. I'm fucking terrified of disappointing him. I'm petrified of something else happening. So all of that rage that stays buried deep down inside ... I decide to unleash it.

"I think you should go," I tell them and my voice is far stronger than I expect. Especially given how much my throat hurts. It doesn't pain me much now; I suppose those drugs are worth the price.

"We have a few more questions first," Hart says.

"Where were you the last two nights?" Barlowe asks.

"Your mother said she looked for you at your place of work and you weren't there. You also weren't at your apartment," Hart adds.

"I'm sorry... what?" Disbelief washes through me, along with a chill from the fever. I feel sick. My poor mother.

There's no way.

"She called asking to file a missing persons report."

My mother spoke to the cops? No fucking way. I don't believe it. My heart thumps and that fucking monitor makes me close my eyes in absolute disdain. I can barely breathe and it takes everything in me not to grab the phone and text her right this minute. I have to keep recording.

Clenching my jaw, I tell them, "Just got a new phone. I'll be sure to text her and let her know I've been under the weather."

"Is there a reason you missed work, haven't been to your residence in forty-eight hours and now you're in the hospital with marks on your wrists and ... what exactly are you here for?" Hart asks.

"None of your fucking business. If I had an orgy in the fucking tundra and got a cold, it's none of your damn business." I emphasize each word and quickly regret being such a bitch.

"I'm sorry, Officers—"

"Detectives," Barlowe corrects and any semblance of niceties leaves me.

"I knew my mother was overprotective but damn, this seems a little much."

"Declan Cross is a suspect in a number of crimes and you have been spotted with him numerous times in the last month," Hart says.

He pauses and silence sits between us. Both of them stare at me and I'm forced to answer, "Is there a question there?"

"Do you have anything you'd like to tell us?" Barlowe asks.

"Your code name, perhaps?" Hart questions.

"Code name?" My voice practically squeaks. "If you mean my *pet name*, he calls me his little fuck toy and I rather like it." The defensiveness raises my voice far too loud. If any hospital staff is outside the door, they undoubtedly hear me. "Please leave me the fuck alone. I don't have anything to say."

"If you have any knowledge of criminal activity pertaining to Declan Cross and you intentionally keep it from us, we'll make sure that you're convicted alongside him," Barlowe says, attempting to intimidate me, but it's useless. They will never get a word out of me.

The battering ram of my heart crashing against my chest is matched by the ridiculous *beep, beep, beep* and I've finally had enough, ripping the sticky electrodes the fuck off.

"I don't consent to a search. I don't consent to shit. And I'm not saying anything else other than, have a pleasant fucking day unless you'd like to detain me."

A beat passes and then another. All the while, I stare at the wall rather than them. There's no more beep, no sound at all other than the blood rushing in my ears.

It's then that Declan comes in and I've never felt such relief.

"If that's all, ma'am," Barlowe says and they leave; Hart doesn't say a word.

With a plastic bag in one hand, Declan watches them as they each pass, one on each side of him.

I'm so damn grateful I tore the monitors off, because if it was on right now, the beeps would give away how fast my heart is racing.

Declan continues toward me, a scowl on his face as he watches the men leave.

I swallow thickly and the moment the door closes I shove the phone into Declan's chest.

"I recorded everything," I tell him, my words rushed.

With his left hand, he holds his phone to his chest. With his right, he offers me the bag. "I got you soup."

I'm hesitant to take it. He heard me, didn't he? I have it all fucking recorded. They can't say I said anything. I have it. I have it all on the phone he gave me. I stare at it, willing him to just look.

"They upset you?"

"They asked me questions and I didn't tell them anything."

"Calm down, my little pet."

"I swear, they said my mom called them and that I was missing—"

"Hey, hey," he says and runs a soothing hand down my hair, hushing me as I heave in a breath. "It's okay, they're gone."

"I didn't tell them anything," I stress to him and the back of my eyes prick as I do. Tears threaten to spill out, it's all so overwhelming. "Just listen."

"I believe you," he tells me, staring at me, seeming to see through me.

He kisses me, tenderly and then deeper. My lips mold to his and I want more. I need more, but he pulls away.

"I swear, whatever they tell you, I have it recorded." I try to explain to him.

"I got your red flag text and came as soon as I could."

"I didn't know what to text you and I—"

"You did just fine, my little pet. Perfect even," he tells me and I believe him, yet at the same time, I don't. It can't be that simple. He hasn't even listened yet.

"I'm sorry, I should have had men outside of the room."

"Watch it. I didn't say anything," I try to reassure him.

"I don't have to watch it—"

"I want you to." My voice is louder than I meant it to be. He needs to listen. He needs to know I didn't say a damn thing. "I want you to know—"

"Okay, it's okay," he says in such a calming tone, like he's trying to calm me down more than anything. He concedes, "I'll watch it."

"I don't know that you can see anything, but you can hear it and you saw them." I explain, feeling light-headed and unsure. I did record it. *Didn't I?* I have to look down at my phone, which is still recording. I press end and watch the wheel spin until it's done. It's there. It's right there. "I can prove I didn't say anything," I say and hold it up for him, my heart still racing.

"I believe you, Braelynn," Declan tells me with such sincerity and I didn't realize how much I needed to hear him say it.

He believes me. "I know you wouldn't say anything," he adds. As I stare up at him, full of mixed emotion I can barely contain, he leans down and kisses me. My lips mold to his and my body relaxes instantly. Every inch of me giving into him, feeling safe with him, feeling comforted by his touch. He pulls away far too soon and when he does, he tells me again, "I believe you."

I hold his hand, the one cupping my chin and I don't want to let go of him.

"That's all I needed."

"Let's check with the doctor and see if I can take you home."

"Yes. Please," I tell him and stop myself short of saying I want to go home. I nearly say it, but I don't want him to think I mean my home. I need to go back with him. Right now, I can't be alone and all I want is to be right next to Declan Cross.

Chapter 14

Declan

"Better?" I question and then kiss her inner thigh. Her legs tremble around my shoulders as I prop myself up, the taste of her cunt still on my tongue. I love how she shivers with the lingering effects of her orgasm.

"Yes, Declan," she murmurs, her dark eyes half-lidded with the potent mixture of lust and satisfaction stirring down her body. Her body arches as I toy with her, bringing the tips of my fingers up and down her slit before bending down to suck her clit again. If for no other reason than to hear that low feminine moan and to feel her fingers splaying in my hair, her nails gently scratching my scalp.

I've already fucked her and gotten her off four times. She's sensitized and maybe it's not fair to play with my fuck toy when she's sated beyond reason. When she can barely lift her head.

But it's been three days of her recovering and yesterday was the first time she left this room since I took her to see the doctor. She's mostly slept, and I've either watched her or slept with her ... although it's proven difficult. It's been years since I've taken Sweets to force myself to sleep. We've taken it both nights and I don't think we'll need it tonight. If we do, if she lies awake, tossing and turning with all of those thoughts refusing to be quiet and leave her alone, I'll do what I did the last two nights. I'll kiss her with the drops on my tongue, I'll fuck her into the mattress until she's screaming my name and then I'll sleep beside her, my arm around her waist, her back to my front.

She'll have peaceful, restful, dreamless sleep. Unlike me, she hasn't had a single dream.

I sleep for hours and hours, unable to wake, but reliving nightmares, killing anyone and everyone who tries to touch her. Hooded men, all in black and outnumbering me try to take her from me. Claiming it's necessary, claiming she shouldn't be here. It's a bloodbath in my terrors, but it's heaven to wake up to Braelynn, safe and warm in my bed, kissable, fuckable, and all mine. I wake up with my heart racing and a cold sweat lining every inch of my skin. She's in my arms, though, peacefully sleeping, unaware. As she should be.

That's partly why I've stayed with her, hardly leaving my

room. This past week fucked her up, I know it did. It fucked me up too. The difference is I deserved it.

I want nothing more than for my cock to be hard again and buried inside of her, reminding her of just how fucking good I am to her.

Just as I'm about to slip three fingers into her, curve my fingers and strum her G-spot, my phone buzzes again on my nightstand.

Annoyance threatens to take over as I sit up enough to see that it's Carter. Lying beside me, Braelynn's dark pebbled nipples beg me to give them attention too as her hand rises up her body. Her hand gently passes her breasts and she lifts her head slightly, to push her hair back, away from her face. Her eyes closed, her movements slow and her legs clenching with the heated need for release.

I've oversensitized my sweet naïve girl. Rising up on my knees I make a move to reach for my phone, but Braelynn mistakes my effort for something far more enjoyable.

A low groan leaves me as her eyes open and she finds mine while turning to position herself so her lips can wrap around my hardening dick.

Gripping the nape of her neck, I keep her just shy of reaching her goal.

Fuck-me eyes peek up at me. "Not yet," I tell her and then release her, opting to cover her with the covers. "Go run the bath for us," I tell her before turning my attention to the phone.

Braelynn is slow and careful to move, but does as commanded, careful as she slips off the edge, a murmur of sweet pleasure leaving her.

I'll bathe her, feed her, and then fuck her again.

Checking the messages on my phone, I'm resolute in my decision to not force her to come with me to the kitchen. Carter isn't convinced and he's not the only one.

It hasn't escaped me that the terrors are likely because I know the whispers going around. *That she's a rat.* The very thought that men who do my bidding could possibly think she's the enemy stirs a heat inside of me that's uncontainable. It's a rage like I've never felt in my entire life. She didn't fucking do it. I know it in my goddamn bones.

Efforts have been made to pin it on Hale. With my throat tight I read Nate's messages that people are questioning if Hale set her up. Some sympathize with her. Nate and Carter have said they all need to sympathize with her, but I disagree. They all need to fear saying her fucking name at all. She doesn't exist for them. She is only mine.

Gritting my teeth, I reread the prior messages from Carter and his prying questions.

I'd texted him yesterday: *I told you. Something happened, but I don't think she knows exactly what. I don't think she has a clue.*

He responded: *I'm not entirely convinced she wasn't expecting something like the hospital scene.*

The disappointment that came over me, the feeling of failure even, was unexpected. It runs through me just the same as I read the messages again.

Declan: *Do you have another test for her, then?*

Carter: *Not at the moment. I'll think of something.*

His next question, the one that just came in, earns not just annoyance, but an anger that I'm becoming more and more familiar with. *What did she do that left her with a bruised ass if it's not related to this?*

I respond to him without thinking twice: *Nothing that's any of your business.*

It's then that there's a knock on the bedroom door. Gentle and in an easy pattern of three: *knock, knock, knock.*

I'd be surprised if it was Carter behind the door. I'm quick to find my boxers under the pile of clothes left in a puddle on the floor. With a quick glance to the bathroom door that's open, and with the sound of running water, I decide to only open the door just enough as necessary.

With a slight groan of the hinges it opens and I find Jase in a dark gray suit. With a clean-shaven jaw and a charming smile, no one would ever suspect my brother to be as ruthless and cutthroat as he is. I've seen him kill a man for uttering his wife's name. He's fast with a knife, even faster with his temper.

Anyone would fear Carter from a single glance, but Jase could fool the best of them. I know that all too well. It's never made me feel uneasy until this very moment to know that.

"Hey," I greet him and he offers me a stack of boxes.

"These came for you?"

"It's about damn time," I say and accept the boxes, opening the door wider. Jase's first instinct is to look into the room.

"She sleeping?" he questions as he glances to the bed before thinking better of it. I'm almost sure the moment he saw the sheets disturbed he realized she might be less than decent.

"How's she feeling?" He's careful to keep his eyes averted when he asks.

"Better. Much better," I answer and a bit of the unease wanes. It's unmistakable, this shift inside of me. As much as I will never forgive myself for letting her go through that, I find myself shifting the blame to my brothers.

Scratching the back of his head, Jase stares at the door until I tell him she's not there.

"She's in the bath, it's fine." With that, he relaxes somewhat, but as I pile the boxes on the bed, he stays outside of the door.

"I'm guessing these are for her too?"

"Yeah," I answer him, checking the labels. All three of these are from Saks Fifth Avenue. I'm not sure if it's the heels, lingerie, or the clothing that have come in for her. "As much as I love her in my T-shirts, I decided she should wear a bit more around the house."

"You two ever going to come out of there?"

"I thought I was supposed to take off this week and next?"

I remind him. "Or do you need me back."

"You don't need to work ... just ... haven't seen you."

"Wouldn't you spend your vacation in bed?" I say lightly, like there isn't another reason that I've avoided them and stayed with her.

"I'd like to get to know her." His statement brings a prick at the back of my neck and a chill to flow down my shoulders. Again I'm struck by the fact that I've felt this before, but never toward my brothers. Never toward my family. Jase adds in my silence, "Because she means something to you ... right?"

"Yeah, she does," I answer him and shove down whatever the fuck it is that's come over me.

"No rush," he says and shrugs. "We should do dinner this week, though, I think? She could meet Bethany and Aria ... or is it too soon for that?" he questions.

I don't have any answer for him. All I can offer is, "Maybe, I'll let you know."

His expression drops slightly, but he nods and clears his throat. "There are a couple of other boxes in the kitchen too," he tells me although his brow is pinched and his gaze shifts from me to the bathroom where the water has stopped running.

Her bath must be full.

"Thanks for bringing these down," I start and prepare to shut the door, but his hand comes out, stopping it abruptly.

"How are you doing?" Jase asks me.

"I could be better." The honest answer comes from me without my conscious consent.

"I can tell," he answers and then asks, "You need anything?"

With an anxiousness in the pit of my stomach, I lie and tell him, "No, I'm good." With that, he tells me all right and that he'll leave me alone. Shutting the door, regret and even fear both linger.

Adrenaline flows through my veins, pumping my heart harder as I head numbly toward the bathroom. I'm not prepared for the gruesome image that flashes to mind. A bath filled with blood, the deep red line a stark contrast against the pristine white porcelain. Her throat slit just like the man who dared insult Jase's wife. Her black hair floating like a halo along her tan skin and her eyes closed.

"I feel so much better," she murmurs as she shifts in the milky bathwater. In a single blink the vision is gone, my beautiful Braelynn very much alive although sleepy. Steam rises gently from the heated surface of the water.

"Are you coming in?" she asks as I question my sanity and what the fuck has come over me.

Chapter 15

Braelynn

Every doubt that whispered in the back of my mind that Declan doesn't want me anymore has silenced in the last twenty-four hours. He's kissed every inch of my body and last night he held me in the bath as if he were afraid I would leave him.

There's not a piece of me that wants to ever be without him. As fucked up and wrong as it sounds, I desperately love him.

I can't forget what happened, though, and that fear still screams and grips me every single night until Declan gives me medicine to sleep. He tells me those who lied to him are dead and that it will never happen again. He tells me it's done and over with, and not to think of it or ever bring it up. He tells me to forget it.

I don't know how I will ever forget, though.

Those men and that tub will forever be etched into my memory. Even walking into the foyer, knowing one of the sets of double doors leads to that room gives me chills.

As I play with the hem of the cashmere sweater Declan gave me, I pretend none of those doors exist. I don't know for certain which ones lead to his brothers' halls and which is the hall of nightmares, but I ignore them all and that's simply how I'll survive and obey Declan, trying to forget it all.

I make it through the day by staying in a bubble and pretending it's all right. I give him my worries and they're simply gone.

The slippers are so very quiet as I make my way this early morning to the kitchen. Even though I'm finally dressed appropriately, in a cream sweater and black leggings that are the most expensive pieces I'm sure I'll ever own, I still don't want to see anyone else.

Not his brothers or anyone who works for him.

I swallow thickly at the thought as I round the corner and hear voices. *Shit.* My fingers go numb as dread spreads through me. They were kind last time and they may have had nothing to do with what happened; I can't help it, though. Nate knew and worked for Declan. His brothers didn't ask questions about how I got like that in the kitchen. No questions that would make it seem that they didn't know what was going to happen.

Glancing over my shoulder, I contemplate turning back. Heading back empty-handed to the bedroom where Declan is sleeping and waiting for him to wake up. No surprise coffee to greet him with. I can't spoil him like he does me. And spoil me he undoubtedly has.

With his touch and affection, with drawers of new clothes and anything I ask for. He's also kept me to himself, locked in his bedroom. I haven't even ventured into the rooms of his hall nor asked about them. I haven't asked him anything.

A part of me knows it's for the same reason that I don't want to see his family. Questions are going to get me killed, so if I just stay silent, everything will be all right.

My heart beats heavy in my chest. It's a sharp pain almost, and I find myself staring blankly at the threshold to the kitchen, heat overtaking me and my legs feeling weak.

"I don't know how it's going to quiet down about Braelynn."

My blood runs cold as the voices coming from the kitchen get louder. If I could move, I'd take a step back, but I'm paralyzed. *They're talking about me.*

"As long as she doesn't leave—" Jase, I think, starts to answer Daniel's statement.

"They all thought she was a rat, now they think Hale and Ronnie set her up. It's going to take a long fucking time for it to blow over, though, and—" Daniel says.

"Some will never change their minds about her," Carter

comments coldly, with a tone that's absolute.

My heart races as I suck in a sharp breath.

"He'll keep her here until it does. She can't be seen until it dies down, especially not with all of the shit with the feds right now ... Right?" Jase questions and it's quiet. Perhaps someone shrugged; I don't know. The coffee machine is heard and I find myself wishing they would say it's going to be okay. That it's already died down. That they believe me.

Tears prick the back of my eyes. I swear I didn't do it. I didn't. I didn't tell anyone anything.

"He already told her if she doesn't listen, then—" Daniel starts to say. *What? Told me what?*

"Did he tell her that, though? You know Declan ..." Jase's voice quiets and I wonder what they mean. Declan didn't tell me a damn thing other than that it's over. He didn't tell me to stay here. A cold sweat at the back of my neck forms as the realization dawns on me.

The front doors beckon to me. With their etched glass and copper handles, the large double doors offer me a glimpse of freedom. There are iron bars on the other side of the glass and beyond that a gated fence guarded by armed men loyal to the Cross brothers. It takes me a second before I notice the keypad beside the set of doors. Without that code, I'm not going anywhere.

My fingers tremble as I realize I'm trapped. I don't know if I'll ever leave here.

"Hello," a voice states behind me and my heart leaps out of my chest. I'm thankful I don't scream because if I wasn't filling my lungs with the shock of being caught eavesdropping, I would have.

A gentle hand reaches out, landing on my shoulder and I stare wide eyed at a beautiful woman. She's tall with long dark hair, gorgeous hazel eyes and cloaked in a deep red silk robe that skims the floor. In bare feet and not a bit of makeup on, it's obvious that she lives here and I know without asking who she is.

Aria Talvery—now Cross. A chill runs down the length of my spine. It's well known that Carter is cruel and heartless, and they say Aria was made for him, his perfect counter. She destroyed the Talvery mafia, burned it all to the ground when she chose Carter.

Their story sent fear through every street. When she and her men joined the Cross brothers' mob, no one on the East Coast stood a chance. Men who refuted the hold the Cross brothers held were murdered on sight. Hell, four men were murdered one week and their tongues cut out of their mouths for disparaging Aria ... saying she would always be a Talvery.

They rule with fear and murder. Always have and always will.

Although there are other whispers, about the hellish story that brought the two of them together ... I'm not sure what's true or not, though. As I stand in front of her, I don't know a damn thing.

"Are you lost?" Aria questions, her tone somewhat comical. "I'm Aria. You know Carter, correct?"

Nodding, I force myself to answer and tell her, "I'm Braelynn ... I'm with Declan."

"I know," she answers, and her voice is so much softer than I've imagined. I grew up with the Cross brothers when they were the poor kids on the rough side of town. The unfortunate souls who lost their mother and had a drunk for a father. But the Talverys would never set foot in the public schools, they were like royalty. Corrupt and feared, but wealthy beyond imagine.

She straightens her shoulders some as she crosses her arms over her chest. "So you're Declan's girlfriend?" It's then that I see the pearl and diamond necklace that she wears. My God, that must cost a fortune. It takes everything in me not to stare at her chest where the large teardrop-shaped diamond rests.

"Yes," I answer as the voices behind us get louder before someone hushes someone else and then the men are quiet. Their footsteps are anything but.

"Good morning," Daniel greets us easily enough. All the while, as the men pass us, my heart beats wildly and my ears heat as if they're burning. It's odd, to see them all in black silk or flannel pajama pants and not crisp suits. Daniel lifts his coffee cup toward me and I respond with the effort of a smile as much as I can.

"Everything all right?" Jase asks and I'm not sure if he's asking me or Aria but she hums an "mm-hmm" and nods and that suits Jase. He tilts his chin up at me, in a greeting of sorts and lets me know the machine is ready if I need coffee.

"Thank you," is all I manage to say as Daniel and Jase continue toward the open doorway that I think leads to the den, a joint communal area much like the kitchen. I know the closed doors lead to wings, five of them total. One will forever be known as the Hell Hall to me.

"I'll be in my office," Carter murmurs to Aria, an arm wrapping possessively around her waist. He glances at me, the look neutral yet prying, before planting a single kiss on her cheek. It's ... odd, in a way I can't place. A man like him being gentle. A man like him being kind even.

A smile plays on her lips as Aria closes her eyes and then pats his arm, like she's giving him permission to go. "I'll be in there soon," she tells him.

With the farewell, he doesn't follow Jase and Daniel and I find myself watching him as he goes through the doors on the farthest right. The doors to Declan's hall are through the farthest left.

"Did you need help with something? Maybe in the kitchen?"

I need to recover more than anything. To just be alone. I shake my head and tell her I was just going to go back to the bedroom.

"But you haven't even gone to the kitchen yet," she points out. My cheeks flush as she leans forward and whispers, "There are cameras."

A spiked ball forms in my throat as I swallow down the feeling that consumes me once again. That this beautiful place is a prison for me.

"I was going to get coffee for me and Declan."

"And you know how to work the machine?" she questions. I nod without thinking and then I realize that I don't know. I have no fucking clue but I'm not stupid. I can figure it out.

She nods slowly, her eyes never leaving mine and her fingernails play along the pad of her thumb as she searches for something in my expression. "I find it's best not to eavesdrop."

"I wasn't." The words come out of me quickly, dripping with denial and even I know it's a lie.

Aria simply cocks a knowing brow in response. I've never been so intimidated or embarrassed.

"I mean," I say and swallow thickly, my fingers twisting around the hem of my sweater, "I didn't mean to."

She nods again and then her expression turns somewhat sympathetic.

"Are you feeling better?" she asks and my heart pounds.

"Much."

"I'm glad you're well," she says and I can barely whisper my thanks. *She knows.* I think everyone knows.

I have all of these thoughts about her, a woman who's practically a myth. It's dawned on me that she absolutely has an opinion about me. I have no idea what she's heard, but I'm sure none of it is good.

The mix of emotions that sour my stomach must show on my face.

"We're doing construction the next couple of weeks starting tomorrow. It would be easiest to run then," Aria says without warning.

"What?" Every bit of blood feels like it leaves my face and a chill comes over my body. "I'm not planning on running."

"He told you not to leave him?"

"Right," I answer again without thinking and then realize what that truly means.

"But do you want to be locked away here, not allowed to leave unless he gives you permission?"

I can't answer. It's only just now dawned on me that this is my reality.

The sympathy in Aria's expression deepens and I wish I were anywhere else. I've only wanted coffee and instead I've been hit with a wrecking ball.

"Can I give you some advice?" she asks and I nod, swallowing the growing lump in my throat.

"Don't trust anyone," she tells me and then offers a sad smile like it's her way of saying goodbye. "And if you ever leave, run very far and never look back."

My racing heart won't stop. Even with deep breaths and slow-paced steps on the way back to Declan's bedroom, the heavy pounding is met with unease that won't quit.

Even if Declan believes me, they don't. I swallow thickly and I swear all I can hear is my damn heart as I turn the knob to the bedroom door.

It's betrayal that pricks along my skin as I walk in and the door creaks shut behind me.

It's agony, though, when I see him, a smirk plays along his lips when I enter. It doesn't match the rest of his expression at all. The dark undereye circles haven't left him and it's almost as if he's worse off after sleeping.

"You're up," I comment.

"Not before you, though."

I almost ask him if he had another nightmare, but I bite my tongue.

With his white shirt being pulled down his chest I catch a glimpse of his hard body. In pajamas he should seem casual, but there's no doubting what I see in front of me. A man who isn't going to let me go and if ever he does ... I think it will be my last breath.

"For me?" he questions and I don't know how I hold it together. I don't know how I lift the mug up and answer evenly, "Just how you like it."

Inside I am one thing; outside quite another. Every inch of my body chills as his hand brushes mine and he kisses my cheek.

I can't help the fear that consumes me.

"You all right?" he asks, then pulls back and rests his palm against my forehead. Is he feigning concern? I can't tell anymore.

"Just a little light-headed, I think."

"Lie down," he orders, his tone more commanding. *More him.*

The sheets rustle as he pulls them back. I obey, my limbs moving as Declan asks me what I need and what he can get me.

I just want to leave, but I don't dare say it.

"I think I'm just going to call my mom," I tell him, doing my best not to let on to the fact that I'll know she'll want to see me. That she'll push for it. I add, "I don't want her to worry."

"No need," he tells me, moving the comforter up to tuck me in. "I texted her from your phone just a bit ago."

"What?" The whispered word holds more shock than anything else and my damn heart hammers even faster.

"You weren't here and it was going off." He cocks a brow before reaching for the nightstand and handing it to me. His fingers blaze against mine as I take it.

"Just told her that you were feeling better but taking the week off," he tells me as I read the message.

"She went to your place and you weren't there. I didn't

want her to think anything bad had happened to you."

I skim through the messages, a cold prick flowing down my skin as I do.

Mom: *Where are you? Nena, you're scaring me.*

Mom: *I messaged Scarlet and her phone isn't working. No one has seen you or heard from you in a week.*

Mom: *Nena, please just answer me.*

MISSED CALL

Me: *I'm sorry, Mama. I'm on medicine and I was knocked out cold. I'm feeling a lot better. You don't have to worry.*

Mom: *Where are you?*

MISSED CALL

Me: *Just crashing at a friend's until I'm better. I'll call you soon, Mama. Don't worry about me, it's just a cold.*

Mom: *You promise you're all right?*

Me: *I promise. Don't worry about me. I'll be fine.*

Mom: *Te extraño y te amo*

Me: *Te amo.*

"Since when did you learn Spanish?" I half joke to keep it light, to not let on to the terror I feel that he's keeping me from her. My tone doesn't hide a damn thing, though.

He ignores my question and instead asks one of his own. "You don't like that I answered her, do you?"

His sharp hazel gaze pierces through mine and all the blood drains from my face.

"It's okay, Braelynn," he whispers and the bed groans as

he leans over to kiss me. He's gentle and the single act is more comforting than I could have imagined.

He leans back and that charming smirk is on his lips again. "I want to be here when you talk to her, though, do you understand that?"

The comfort vanishes as I swallow thickly and nod. "Yes."

Chapter 16

Declan

The door to Carter's office opens with a creak, announcing my arrival. It was ajar and when he messaged about needing to talk I headed to his wing immediately.

Still, I rap my knuckles on the partially opened door and Carter looks up from his laptop. I swear it's always the same with him. The thick dark curtains are closed behind him. The fireplace is lit and the light leaves a soft glow across the long wall of old books and a shadow across his face.

It's not until he registers it's me that his expression softens. It's quite the opposite of what I feel. Knowing he must want to discuss my Braelynn, I'm already guarded and defensive. I'm positive my expression must reflect that although if Carter sees it, he doesn't let on.

As he leans back, the chair groans and he motions to the wingback in front of him. "It has your name on it," he comments and then reaches for the mug on his desk. He finds it empty, though, and sets the ceramic cup back down.

As I take a seat, he runs a hand down his face before pinching the bridge of his nose.

"You know, Mom always told me you'd give me a run for my money."

"What?" I can't help that the word slips out and a warmth I wasn't expecting comes over me. It's a rare day that we talk about our mother.

Very rare. We don't talk about what life was like before she died and everything changed.

"You were an animal. Climbing on everything. No fear as a toddler."

"Then I grew up," I joke dryly, but my grin doesn't dampen.

Carter huffs a laugh. "You were her favorite and I—"

"I was her baby boy, but she loved us all." I can almost hear her saying it, calling me her baby boy.

The memory of my mother makes the tips of my fingers go numb and I find myself tapping them against the leather armrest. My mother loved us more than anything and she would have done anything for us. But the last years of our life she spent sick and on bed rest. I can barely remember a moment with her where she wasn't succumbing to her cancer. The rest of my brothers can, though. They remember things I don't. We all remember our father, though, and how he turned into a different man when she died. In a lot of ways, he died with her.

"I remember one day," Carter says, leaning back and staring past me at the back wall, "she said that when she was gone, that you were the one who would give me a run for my money."

I let out a huff, knowing damn full well Daniel is the one who we all had to keep close. But that's for an entirely different reason. When he left, for a long time I thought he might never come back. That was a dark time for us all.

"You were her favorite," Carter says as if he's reminiscing. All of my brothers say that, but I know she loved us all.

"Is that why you called me in here?" I ask him with a smirk although I'm not feeling jovial. I'm more anxious than anything after leaving Braelynn. For her, I crossed a line messaging her mother on her behalf. For me, she needs to realize things have shifted to be sharper than before. There's a number of things she's going to be uncomfortable with and the sooner we get that situated, the better.

"It's about Braelynn," he tells me and I huff a humorless laugh, running a hand through the back of my hair. "Of course it is," I answer. "I told you, it's taken care of."

"She's scared, Declan."

"No shit—" I almost remind him how out of fucking touch he is. How all of this is a shock to her. How even his own wife once had a more difficult time coping than Braelynn is right now ... and Aria grew up in the life.

"I don't want to fight. This isn't me coming for her or getting in between you two. I'm trying to help ... to find a way for ..."

"For what?"

"For both of you to be happy and ... she's fucking terrified."

My tone is harsh when I tell him, "She needs time; she'll be fine." My throat dries as I stare down my brother. She is *mine*. They can't take her away from me. Although my hackles are raised, his aren't.

"Aria told me they had a conversation," he confesses. Slight shock and, to my surprise, betrayal flicker through me. *Why wouldn't she tell me?*

"Did she tell you?"

"No," I answer and I readjust in the seat uncomfortably. "She didn't tell me."

"It wasn't long, but Aria let me know." Braelynn didn't tell me. Why the hell wouldn't she tell me?

"What did they talk about?"

All manner of things race through my mind. The one question I've just asked Carter, though, screams that I don't have the control over Braelynn I thought I did and that's dangerous. It's a dangerous thing for her to be in my world, but to not confide in me. To have secrets even.

"Aria didn't say exactly. She just said she was obviously

not well and reluctant to say anything at all."

"I think that's not unreasonable. She needs time to adjust. Aria of all people should know that." Every word falls flat and I'm certain Carter can see through it. The mention of his wife brings a touch of tension to his posture.

It's quiet a moment, not a sound other than the steady ticking of the grandfather clock in the corner of his office and the crackle of the fire.

"Braelynn will get used to it — just like we all did. We all adjusted."

"Why not give her an out?" Carter suggests and instantly I hate it.

"What do you mean?" I barely speak the menacing question.

"Offer her a way out where she can leave all of this behind and know that she's safe."

"Leave me, you mean?" I'm ashamed of how my voice cracks. Of how he could possibly turn his back on me. Break his fucking word to me that she is mine to do with as I see fit.

"You can always bring her back," Carter says, rushing the words out. As if they're an excuse for his proposal to be justified. "It's just a way to see—"

"Another test." The hard words leave me with as much anger as they do anguish.

It's quiet, far too quiet and I lift my gaze back up to Carter to see him nod.

"Another test but also ... an option for space."

A sarcastic huff of a laugh leaves me and I tell him bluntly, "She doesn't need space." I practically spit the words. She needs protection and a firm hand, and he knows that.

I'm struck by the softness in his tone as he tells me, "If I could go back, I would have given Aria more space. I would have let her adjust more comfortably."

A moment passes and then another as I let his words sink in.

"You did give her space," I point out, remembering all too well.

"After too much shit happened ... after it was almost too late."

"It all worked out in the end. Didn't it?"

"Yes. Yes it did, and I'm grateful it did ... but Aria is also from the life. Braelynn isn't."

"What does that have to do—"

"You know damn well it matters. She doesn't know shit about how to navigate our world."

My thumb runs a circle on the pad of my middle finger as I comment lowly, "She'll learn." I wish I could confide in him about the thoughts that plague me when sleep evades me. How almost every night, I witness her die. My own death comes shortly after. It's only a dream, racing thoughts and fears transformed into events that don't exist. But that reality feels so close. As if it's only a single incident from being real.

"I'm scared for her and for you, Declan." I meet my brother's gaze, forcing the fears of my night terrors down. "I mean it, Declan. I'm only trying to help you." I know he'd sacrifice his life for me. I know he would never lead me astray. Deep inside, I know his intentions are pure. Not an ounce of me likes it, though. He's a ruthless, coldhearted man with a reputation of selfishness and callousness. Except for us. Except for family.

With the unsettled feelings stirring, I humor him. "So what are you thinking?"

"A chance to leave, enough money to get away ... a tracker."

"If she takes it, it could mean she did it," I state as if that's the real point to all of this. Knowing Carter, he won't quit until he has an explanation for what occurred. He won't leave it alone. He'll never trust her. He'll never fully bring her in. The realization is a knife to my heart and I can barely listen as he says, "If she takes it, we can watch to see what she does with it."

I'm silent, letting the reality sink in.

He adds, "Who she contacts. It could give her space to adjust to this life on her own terms."

I respond with the only thing I know is true in this moment. "I don't want to give her the option to leave."

"Tell her you don't want her to. So she knows how you feel, but give her the option regardless."

The option. A sickness churns in my gut. She'll take that

option and he knows it. In this moment, I hate him.

"Tell the guards to let her through if she leaves — we'll watch her and follow."

I'm quick to answer him, "It's not going to happen."

His thumb taps absently on the desk. "I hope you're right," he answers.

I don't hide the defensiveness as I bite out, "I am."

The large antique grandfather clock ticks away steadily, the air thick with tension.

"I think I failed you back then. With Mom. It was ... heavy, too heavy." Carter's remark is met with silence. "And I think I may have failed you these last years," he says with genuine remorse.

I can barely think about him and his feelings when he's trying to push away the one woman I have ever loved. I've never asked him for anything. I've given my fucking life to this family. She is all I've ever wanted.

"Declan, no matter what happens, I'm here for you. I will do whatever you think is best when it comes to Braelynn."

"And if I don't want to do this?"

"Then we don't. It's as simple as that." A shred of relief breaks up the tension in my shoulders and I feel as though I can breathe for the first time since he told me Aria and Braelynn talked.

"Above all else, we are blood and I will always protect you."

I answer without hesitation. "Same." Even on the days

I've hated this life, I've loved my brother. That's a truth that I can't ever see changing.

Time passes as I consider everything. As every possibility plays out in my mind.

"Will you leave her alone when she doesn't take it?" I ask him and I nearly said "if," not when. I hate that I almost questioned it.

"If she doesn't take it, even though she has a clear way out," he says and taps his foot once again, "I think she ..."

"What? Say it."

"She doesn't come from this world. If she stays, she would be staying for you."

"When she stays," I correct him.

"When ... when she stays. And everyone would know, she loves you and she isn't leaving."

I nod, meeting his level gaze.

Braelynn will stay. She knows it's best. She knows I'll protect her. She loves me. She will stay.

Chapter 17

Declan

An hour passes and then another while I sit alone in the kitchen, monitoring the cameras in the bedroom. Half of me expects her to call her mother or do anything other than what's she's done. She's lying in bed, reading a book, occasionally looking at the door.

I know she's waiting for me but I'm not ready to confront her yet. There's truth in what Carter said. Perhaps I haven't locked her in a cage, but Braelynn is my prisoner in a way and she knows it. There's no way she doesn't realize it to some degree.

No amount of emails piling up and even more missed calls can distract myself from that nagging truth in the back of my mind. Even notices from the FBI and emails from the district attorney don't carry enough weight to stray my thoughts away from Braelynn.

With the anxiousness building I delete message after message and email after email. Time off is only time piled up. Half of these messages could be ticking time bombs and I couldn't fucking care less.

Jase said he'd step in, but it's been years since anyone else has handled these matters. The last time I sent someone else to take my place, the received message was that of disrespect. It's Jase, though, not Nate. Nate showing up to settle ... issues, speaks one thing loud and clear: it's not worth my fucking time. That's one of the reasons why it's better for me to handle everything myself. The control, the presence, the authority even are better suited for my position. More than once I've attempted to bring Nate in, to take on meets and step up to this position. Not a single time was it received well. For one reason and one reason only, I'll be condemned to this hell for as long as I live—I'm a fucking Cross brother.

Nate's not. He's much like Seth and a few others in our family. He's a longtime friend who's proved his loyalty time and again, and therefore earned his reputation and power. Whenever my brothers had to step away in the past, he stepped up. I couldn't have fucking survived without him there.

Still ... he's not one of us and never will be.

Neither is Braelynn.

Carter's plan, this choice he wants to present to Braelynn,

is a fool's errand. She's not one of us ... yet. And I can't allow her to prove that fact so very clearly to us all. I can't and I won't.

Turning off my phone and pocketing it, I wish I could rid these thoughts but everything comes back to her and what everyone will think. What they'll say. Scenario after scenario plays out in my head as I make my way back to her.

The thud of my footsteps become louder and louder as I get closer. There is only one way that this ends with limited bloodshed: Nate spreads the whispers that the other men betrayed me and she took the fall for it until I found out the truth. All the men, allies and enemies alike believe it. And Braelynn remains loyal and close to my side.

Any other alternative and it all unravels. In this life, that means threats and death, arrests and even war. Everyone is always waiting for a weak moment. We've been through it time and time again.

The men will believe what I've told them. And she will be my perfect submissive. There is no other outcome I'll accept.

With the need to control every single aspect of this fuckup, I open the door and then close it behind me with more anger than intended.

A short gasp from Braelynn and those gorgeous dark wide eyes pinned to me elicits a response from me that's unexpected.

I feel sorry for her. I'm full of guilt that I brought her into this and sorry that she doesn't have a choice anymore.

"It's just me," I offer her in a rough tone as the emotions war inside of me.

With the blanket pulled up her chest and those wide eyes staying large and beautiful, she doesn't answer beyond a short nod.

Carter's right. She's scared. It's not something that's easily ignored. The floorboards creak as I walk to the bed. The only thing she needs to be scared of is disappointing me. The bed groans as I sit at the end of it, frustrated with every fucking thing about this situation. I don't want to be hard on her. With everything she's been through and the hell storm that's coming, I don't want to cause her more pain or fear.

"Is everything okay?" she whispers after a moment of my silent contemplation.

"You know that I care for you and that I want to keep you safe, don't you?" I question without turning to look her in the eyes.

The flickering of scenes from horrid nightmares makes me run a hand down my face. *Care for her* seems so weak compared to what I truly feel. I can barely sleep anymore without watching her die. The thought of losing her is torture.

With nearly sleepless nights filled with terrors, the whispers of men I can't control and Carter's reckless plan, all I can think is that she has to know I did this for her. That if only she listens, I can fix it all.

Desperation isn't an emotion I'm privy to, but it clings to

me when it comes to her. For days now, it's a constant. Does she feel it too?

Finally, I lie down, my feet still planted on the floor and my head by the curve of Braelynn's waist. She doesn't join me initially. "Do you know my mom loved my dad and he loved her too?" I ask her. "You never met them, did you?" I speak without thought. Letting it all come out as it wishes. It can't be any more reckless than what Carter suggested. I'm not aware that I'm holding my breath until she lies down beside me and her warmth wraps itself around me.

"I saw your father once."

"Before or after my mom passed?"

"After."

"He unraveled when she died. He was a better man when she was alive."

Silence sits between us for a moment as she struggles to respond. Finally she admits, "I heard things."

"What kind of things?" I question as I stare up at the ceiling fan with its revolving blades.

"He beat you. He used drugs and had Carter sell them."

"He was an alcoholic and an abusive motherfucker."

"I'm sorry." The air between us is thick with remorse and uncertainty.

"I don't want to lose you, Braelynn—I don't know what I'll become if you leave me." I spit out the confession, giving her a side of me I don't like to admit exists. It's only for her and surely if she knows that, she'll understand.

It's quiet. Quiet for far too long before she murmurs a question she already knows the answer to.

"Am I ... allowed to leave here? I don't want to leave you. I just ... I need to call my mother and I haven't because she'll ask to meet and I don't know if I can."

I don't answer immediately. Instead I swallow, knowing damn well she's eager to leave because she's scared. Just like Carter said. It's a knife to my chest.

"And I need to go home and—" she starts and I cut her off.

"I'd rather you didn't right now." My tone is firmer, more heartless as I remove the desperation in favor of control. *I tried, my Braelynn.* At least I can say I tried. She might hate me for having a stern hand with her for now, but at least she'll be alive at the end of this.

"It doesn't mean forever—just for right now, I want you to stay." *I'll give you every reason to stay.*

Rolling over to my side, I'm met with the sight of her breasts, the thin shirt barely covering them. At the very thought of being more demanding with her, more stern and even brutal if she were to disobey has my cock hardening. Reaching up to the thin fabric, I pluck one of her nipples and the stifled moan and shudder she gives me intensifies my growing need.

"You're scared," I say and peer up at her.

"Yes." The bed groans as my weight shifts and I push

her shoulder down, forcing her to lie beneath me as I slowly tower over her.

"You need to listen to me and do what I say, and that means staying here for a while." I murmur the command as I pull the covers down and then lift up the hem of her shirt. With the chill air, her nipples harden. She doesn't protest in the least, although she questions, "I'm not allowed to leave at all?"

"You're safe here and so you will stay here." After the blunt answer, I lower my lips to her nipples and alternate sucking on each, then nip at her full breasts. Her eyes go half-lidded but her mind is elsewhere.

"Tell me what you're thinking about," I command her.

"Are they going to kill me?" she asks and then she swallows thickly. It seems we're both at war internally. Which isn't fair. This mess is for me to clean up. I've already told her that.

"You will listen to me," I order her as my thumb tears through the fabric at her hips. I pull it away, and lift her thighs up so that my hips sit where I want them between her legs. My cock is eager to punish her pussy for once again defying me.

"If anyone else ever touched you," I answer lowly and test the weight of her breasts before kneading them and kissing her tender flesh, "I'd kill them slowly. They'd die in agony and regret."

She inhales a shuddered breath, and lust heats between us. Her head falls back and I take my time, letting the tips of my fingers slip along her soft skin, leaving goosebumps that I then kiss away.

"I already told you, not a soul will touch you so long as you listen to me and obey," I remind her, and the threat of what will happen if she makes me tell her again is on the tip of my tongue, but instead of uttering the words, I find myself kissing her instead. Her lips part for me, her legs wrapping around my own. She is weak for me when I am strong for her. She is desperate for me as I am for her, but only when I demand it.

All of this is my fault for being weak when it comes to her. I've made my decision. I want her but the only side she's allowed to see is the one where I dominate her, where she doesn't have a choice. It's the side of me she both wants and needs.

"You are mine, aren't you?"

"Yes."

"My sweet naïve girl, that's all you'll ever be, won't you?"

"Yes, Declan."

And you love me, don't you? I almost question. But I stop myself and instead ask, "And you're never going to leave me, are you?" I stroke my cock once and then press my head between her slick slit.

"Never. I won't leave unless you tell me to." The words rush from her as I tilt her hips slightly, gripping just under her ass, hard enough to bruise.

"That's my good girl," I murmur at the shell of her ear and

then thrust into her. Fuck. Her cunt is heaven. Tight and welcoming as I fuck her as deep as I can, taking my time with every thrust.

As I groan into her neck, letting the pleasure ride through me, I catch a glimpse of my beautiful Braelynn. Her eyes closed in rapture, her lips parted in pleasure.

This is all we need. I rock against her, knowing that she loves it. That she fucking loves me and everything I do to her. As I quicken my pace, she attempts to muffle her moans with the sheet and I'll be damned if I let that happen.

Fisting the sheet, I rip it away from her. "Don't you dare, my little fuck toy. Let me hear you." With my hand on her throat, my thumb at her chin forcing her to stare back at me, I fuck her harder and deeper. Her nails dig into my shoulders as she clings to me, moaning my name as I bring her closer and closer to the edge we're both desperate to fall from.

My name.

Mine. Because she's mine.

"You should have given her an out." My eldest brother's voice echoes as he stands in front of the door.

"It was too much for her." Jase's sorrow is heard but I can't see either him or Carter. There's only the door I know in my gut leads to her. Where the tub was. Where they tortured her. A prick at

the back of my neck chills me to my core when I try to listen and hear nothing.

It's only the drip, drip, drip *of the water spilling over.*

"I told you to give her time," Carter tells me and I turn violently to face him, to warn him to leave us alone. With my jaw clenched and anger taken over the deepening fear, I still when there's nothing there. Only an empty hall.

Thump, thump, thump ... *all I can hear is my heart.*

A cold sweat lines the back of my neck as I face the door again.

"Braelynn?" I call out her name as I twist the freezing cold knob. "I told you to stay," I grit out as the door creaks open, only to regret it. I regret it all.

One step forward and I can't go any farther. My knees collapse. Braelynn...

Her small body dangles just feet above the floor.

"You should have given her an out," Carter says from behind me.

"Declan?" I jolt awake, a cold sweat covering every inch of my skin as I shoot up. Braelynn's gasp is met with her pulling the sheet up closer around her as she leans away from me. Wide eyed and terrified. My sweet girl who always smiled, who was playful and mischievous. How long has it been since I've seen her with anything other than this look of caution and fear on her face?

"I'm sorry," she whispers. "You were having a nightmare."

It takes me a moment to compose myself. To swallow and

breathe. To realize it was just another fucking night terror.

I nearly tell her to go to bed. But a different question leaves me instead. "Are you afraid of me?"

She only hesitates for a moment as the late-night light from the moon filters through the blinds and lays across her small body. "You know I am."

Her honesty is quietly spoken.

Mine nearly stays buried inside of me, but this hour of the night leaves no moments for the unspoken needs. "Do you love me?" I ask her.

"Yes," she answers and doesn't hesitate.

"More than you're afraid of me?"

I'm met with silence and her gorgeous deep brown eyes begging me to take that question back. It's all the answer I need.

"Go to sleep, Braelynn," I tell her as I lie back down, unsure of how I can possibly sleep after that. Visions of the night terrors plague me as I lie as still as can be, willing a dreamless sleep to come. It's nearly 5:00 a.m. when my phone lights up with a silent message.

It's from **Carter:** *The cash is here and security has been informed. Whenever you're ready, just let me know.*

CHAPTER 18

BRAELYNN

One wrong move and I'm dead. That's all I keep thinking.

The ice bath and my screams. Aria's warning. Even the way his brothers look at me haunts me every second I'm alone.

I'm terrified to be alone. He knows it. I know that he knows I am. He denies it, and tells me what a good girl I am for listening to him. But inside I'm dying. I know that I'm not okay and I'm too afraid to tell him.

It's been two days since I've spoken to Aria and two nights since Declan confirmed I'm a prisoner. Two days of simply being and the only moments I feel alive are when he's inside of me, holding me and fucking me like he loves me and wants nothing more than me.

Then he leaves me here, alone, with books I can't read

because the words can't be heard over the thoughts screaming in my head. With thoughts and doubts that torment me. Memories of Scarlet and her betrayal, but also her friendship. I knew her for years. I witnessed her die ... only to come close to death myself.

I love Declan Cross and I think I always have, but he's going to be the death of me. I think he knows it too and that's why last night I woke up to him crying out my name.

He knows one day they're going to kill me. It doesn't matter if he loves me too. I'm almost certain of that. I can still feel him pulsing inside of me as pleasure ripples through my body, and yet, all I can think is that I'm never going to leave this place alive.

Part of me wants to drown in sleep medication until all of this is nothing but a memory. Until I'm allowed to leave and be my own person again. My phone sits untouched and I know there are messages from my mother all left unread. I can't lie to her but I can't disobey Declan either. The only thought that screams in my head when I'm left alone is the moment Declan no longer wants me, he'll have me taken care of.

And then he holds me, he kisses me, he makes love to me and it's all soothed away. For only a moment, for only a night. Then I wake up and I'm reminded of the fact that I'm trapped all over again. I wish he would just tell me the truth. I wish I could ask him without being scared that I'll upset him. I thought being with him made me strong, but I'm nothing under him. I'm pitiful and ashamed. Thoughts stray back to my ex and I hate that somehow I feel less now than I did then. I don't know how this happened but I wish Aria hadn't told me so bluntly. I know it's foolish to live in ignorance, and I would have found out and Declan had already crossed a line … I wish I could let it go, but I am unraveling.

I know what it's like to spiral. I've been here before and I'm not okay.

I wish I knew if he really loved me or if he's simply deciding what piece in the game I am and where he's going to put me. I wish I knew how this was going to end.

The one thing I wish more than anything was that I wasn't so desperately in love with him and weak for him but I think I always have been.

The bedroom door opens without warning and my heart attempts to leap out of my chest.

As it batters inside of me, I realize it's only Declan.

Still, my nerves are unsteady. With what looks like a very heavy black duffle bag on one arm, he strides in and dumps it onto the dresser.

I've barely moved from the bed. And as he stands there, as if he's waiting for me, I pull the covers up tighter around myself.

"Declan?" My gaze moves to the bag as he unzips it and the sound fills the room. Nerves prick all over my body. Something's wrong. It's in his posture, in the silence. He doesn't answer, he doesn't give any attention at all to my nervousness. Instead he pulls back the fabric and reveals stacks of cash. I don't have any idea how much it is, or if it's even real. From the bed, I haven't the faintest clue, all I know is that he's staring at it rather than me.

The bed creaks as I shift on it, calling out his name again. "Declan?"

He swallows so hard, I can hear it.

My gaze moves from him, to the cash and back up to him, his sharp gaze piercing into me. Instantly I'm hot all over. The intensity is all too much.

He stalks toward me and it doesn't make any sense that the closer he is, the more comfort I feel. Even when he looks at me like that.

He stops just short of the bed, only inches from me. He could touch me if he wanted.

"Will you kiss me?" he questions.

I answer in the only way I desire, by sitting up on my knees and pressing my lips to his. It's a balm to my soul. The moment his lips meet mine and his hands wrap around my waist, every nerve is soothed. Every fear is forgotten when he kisses me back.

It's okay. It's all going to be okay. The thoughts don't last long, with his grip on my upper arms as the chill of the air comes between us.

When I peer up at him, his hazel eyes are closed for a moment too long.

He's quiet as he pulls back, his fingers in my hair.

"Declan, what's going on?" I barely manage in a whisper. "You're scaring me."

"We'll be leaving," he finally tells me and I almost ask where we're going. Including myself in the statement but I was wrong to assume. I thought maybe, for a split moment, he would take me away. We would run together. My foolish heart. We were never destined to simply be together. Not in this life.

"If you want out of this, you run while we're out."

"What?" My disbelief coats the single word.

"You go wherever you want. Don't tell a soul anything, just stay away and I will let you run."

A numbness creeps inside of me as he pulls back, out of my reach and leaving me there, gripping the edge of the bed like it's only there to hold me steady. "What are you saying?"

"It's a way out for you, Braelynn."

"Declan, stop," I beg him. But he doesn't. He keeps telling me there's enough cash to run and be safe.

As if I could be okay without him. My throat tightens and I can't take it.

"Stop," I tell him as the world seems to close in on me. He tells me about security allowing me to leave. "Stop," I say louder but he doesn't. He tells me my car and the keys are just beyond the kitchen and that the front door will stay open all week while they prepare for construction. "Red!" I safe word, yelling it across the room and he stills.

Finally he silences himself.

My heart races and all I know is that I'm not okay.

He wants me gone.

"Please take it back," I say, barely getting the choked words out. He swallows thickly, but he doesn't do it. Standing between myself and the money, the man I loved, says nothing.

"Please—just—love me." The pathetic plea leaves me.

The word love hangs in the air. He knows that I love him and I know that men like him don't love. They survive the damage they cause and then they keep going.

"I need you to understand, my naïve girl, this is for you."

Shaking my head, I deny that I need this. Running away from him. Stealing his money and hiding ... that's not something I need.

All I can think is to let every and any thought escape me. To be honest with him. I don't want to run. He just doesn't understand. I don't even know if I understand. But this isn't what I want or need.

"I'm afraid of disappointing you and you forcing me to go or me being so afraid that—"

"You know what I think when I think about you? Every mistake I've made. I think about every way I could change this shit we're in." He sounds almost angry with himself as he runs his hand down the back of his hair. The shadows in the room make the curve of his jaw sharper, the bags under his eyes darker. They make him seem even more tormented than he is.

"I'm sorry," I whisper and my voice breaks.

"Why are you sorry? I care about my mistakes because I want to be perfect for you. I'm not, though, Braelynn. I never have been good enough."

I tell him as I crawl slowly to the end of the bed to be closer to him, "I've fucked up. And I know it and I'm sorry. I don't want to leave you." He doesn't move closer to me, though.

"This is an out—"

"Stop!" I scream and then lower my voice to add, "Please … I said red!"

My heart rages as his expression shifts to one of remorse and sympathy. He takes the few steps to meet me at the end of the bed, gently laying his forehead against mine to whisper, "Maybe I should shut the fuck up and just kiss you."

"You should," I tell him, gripping both of his wrists and keeping his hands on me. Don't let go of me and don't let me go, I beg inwardly, but I'm too chickenshit to say it out loud when he peers down at me and his lips find mine.

His touch is no longer a balm. It feels too much like a goodbye.

"I don't want you to leave me. I want you to stay. It won't be like this forever."

"Like what?" I ask him without thinking.

"You know what," he tells me and I do, so I only nod.

"I have to go," he says and pulls his hands away, breaking the grasp I have on him.

"I don't want you to leave me alone."

"You're safe here. I have a lot of things to take care of. A lot has gotten out of hand."

"I'm begging you, please don't leave right now."

"I have to. You're going to be my good girl."

He tells me like it's a statement and I don't know what he means. I don't know what he wants from me. All I know is that I'm not okay.

"You don't want me to leave?"

"It would destroy me if you did," he confesses to me. "But I—"

"Then I won't," I say, cutting him off. My heart still races, but with our gazes locked I know exactly what this is. It's a test. "I won't leave you. I promise."

For the first time since he came in here, his lips lift slightly, in the saddest of smiles.

With his thumb running down my jaw he murmurs, "That should make me happy ..."

He doesn't say the "but it doesn't," part aloud, but I hear it anyway.

Chapter 19

Declan

If I could calm the fuck down, this would go by easier. I'm nervous as fuck and with the way my foot keeps tapping against the table leg and how often I readjust in my office chair, everyone in this room knows it.

My family's main lawyer, Michael McHale, plus Carter and Nate. Forcing out a steady breath, I do everything I can to focus as Carter's hand comes down on my shoulder.

As if that will be enough to bring me back to the conversation.

They continue to discuss the possibility of a deposition or facing charges now that they've ruled Scarlet's disappearance a murder. How the fuck that happened, I don't know. I don't even fucking care. My gaze continues to drift to my phone that's facedown on the desk.

I could so easily flip it over and watch her. All I want to know is whether or not she's going to take the out. It's fucking killing me.

Don't leave me, Braelynn.

How fucking selfish of me to want her to stay when I know I should have never touched her. The photograph of Scarlet that aired on the local news last night is placed down in front of me. She's younger in the picture than when she started working here; that much is obvious from a glance at her fresh face with no makeup and her hair pulled back. Smiling and celebrating completing basic field training.

Remorse and regret spark a dull flame that's quickly extinguished. She knew what she was doing and she knew there were only two ways for it to end.

And she brought my Braelynn into this.

"They aired that she's believed to be dead although her body hasn't been found."

"On what basis?" Carter questions.

"They announced they had clear persons of interest who were potential suspects, but we haven't received or heard anything from the DA."

"How soon can we expect to be questioned?" Nate asks. I've known him for years and I know his tells. He's anxious and for good reason. He's the one who disposed of her. If he fucked up anything, they'll be able to pin on it him first.

"It depends on how the deposition in the—"

"Who's being deposed?" Carter asks for clarification.

"Nate first." At the confident declaration, a quiet Nate meets my lawyer's gaze and nods in understanding. "Then we can expect them to make the rounds until they've gone through every employee."

"Working from the bottom to the top," Carter comments dryly and then leans back in his seat. I'm at the head of the desk with Carter beside me. Nate is seated across to our right and Michael is to our left. While we're all in suits, Nate wears a thin tie, our lawyer a bow tie and Carter and I have none. My sleeves are rolled up to my forearms and without my jacket and not having shaved since yesterday, I'm certainly the least professional-looking one in the room.

"Anything in particular I can expect in questioning?" Nate asks.

"If it's just being hauled in for questioning, demand a lawyer and don't say shit," I tell him.

"I meant deposition," Nate clarifies. It'll be his first if they go through with it.

The cops arrested one of the men who work here, Bardot, and the DA brought charges of drug trafficking. Now they're using that to force every single person who's worked for us to testify under oath in a deposition.

It's not the first time we've been through this shit. Won't be the last.

But given the murmurs and questioning around first Scarlet, then Ronnie, then Hale ... loyalty is questionable.

"I'll be there and object to anything and everything. Don't answer without a nod from me. I don't care what they ask; until I nod, you stay silent." Our lawyer is a shark and we still have a firm grip on enough of the DA's office that it's not too concerning.

So all of this is simply eating up the time between now and the moment I check to see if Braelynn is waiting for me.

"We should talk about the girl," McHale brings up and my gaze is quick to move from the hardwood desk to his pale blues behind wire-rimmed glasses.

"Is she all right?" he asks. I know the hidden question behind those four words. *Is she dead?*

"She's fine," I answer over Carter who opened his mouth to speak. Pushing my sleeves up further, I ignore the prick at the back of my neck and all the nerves on high alert at the mere thought of her being pulled into this. Now is not the time to let her run. I was the one who pulled the trigger to get it over with. I only pray I haven't fucked up everything even more than I already have.

"Does her family know that?" he asks. "Her mother has been calling around and even showed up at The Club looking for her."

"When was that?"

"A few days ago."

"She's been texting her mom. She's fine, was just sick for a moment."

My lawyer's stare is that of a man who's used to reading between the lines.

Scowling, I tell him, "She was actually sick. A cold or something. She's better now but resting up. I'm doing what I can to spoil her given how she's had a difficult couple of weeks."

"So she's good?" he asks, his brow raised.

"She's good," Carter declares.

"Would she be good if she was brought in for questioning?" McHale questions and anger heats every inch of me. She needs to stay out of this.

"Scarlet was her friend, right? She was seen with her the week she died?"

"You would be there if she was questioned or deposed, so she would be fine," Carter says to me and it's silent a moment. Michael's reading between the lines of what Carter is suggesting.

My head spins with the possibility of her in questioning. It's too fucking risky. All of it is.

"What about E?" McHale continues. He's referring to a business associate of ours. His real name is Ian, but for some fucking reason he goes by E.

When Bardot got arrested and didn't show up for work ... it caused a bit of a stir. E doesn't have time or patience. He doesn't work for us but it's to our benefit to keep business flowing with E in upstate New York.

"We'll get him what he needs. He knows this kind of thing is just part of the game."

"He's anxious and for good reason, but I'll reach out and smooth things over. Reassure him that everything is fine," Carter answers, shifting slightly in his seat and I'm almost certain it's the only move he's made for the last twenty minutes.

"Any word from Marcus?"

"He's still quiet," Carter answers and a cold chill runs down my spine.

"Quiet isn't bad," Michael suggests.

"In the case of Marcus, it's not good either."

There are far too many players, and far too many power moves going on at once for me to be distracted by Braelynn. Yet she's all I can think about. What she does next is the only thing that seems to matter.

All I keep picturing is her in that room, knowing she has an out and taking it. Fuck, if she knew everything, she'd be smart to leave me.

"Declan?" Michael's tone prods me from my thoughts back to the present where three sets of eyes bore into me with concern. Waiting for a response. "Did you hear me?"

Clearing my throat I shake my head slightly and wait for my lawyer to repeat whatever he said.

"We were given a heads-up that the officer in charge is working with a judge who isn't in our back pocket."

"Right. We knew he probably would."

"So, prepare for questioning. Nate first, but they're more than likely planning to pick you up and you should decide where you want that to happen. Here? In The Club, or at home or ... let me know so I can plant that seed."

This isn't the first time I'll be picked up by the cops for questioning. It's the first time that I've thought about who will be with me when they do, though.

What she'll see and what she'll think. And who will be there for Braelynn if it's just the two of us and they take me away.

"Let me know," McHale prods for an answer and instead of giving him a time and place, I hesitate and let him know I'll get back to him.

I need to take care of her first. I can't handle all of this shit without knowing if she's even going to be there. I take a glance at my brother as every thought of what she'd do if they pulled her in for questioning races in my mind and I find his gaze on me just the same.

It's unsettling. Every detail we've gone over feels like it could be the one that ends us.

Chapter 20

Braelynn

I haven't touched the money yet. Although I stare at it from the bed and even as I stand here, in front of the dresser while I slip on black leggings that feel like silk and an oversized soft wool sweater, I can smell it.

Declan said the stacks added up to over a million. And it sits there, only inches away.

Letting out an uncomfortable sigh, I stare at the door and wish I were anywhere else. I wish I could simply go home or go to my mother's.

This room is a test, this estate is a trap and it's like I'm playing mind games with the devil every minute that ticks by.

The one question every decision seems to ride on is whether or not he loves me. Does Declan love me?

It feels like he does when he's with me but sometimes it also feels like he's testing me, like he's waiting for me to fail and I know that's not love. This could all be a sick twisted game for him. There is so much more darkness to Declan than I know. I'm all too aware he's done things that would chill me to my core. Can a man like that truly love anyone? Let alone me?

My heart aches questioning it. Because I love him. Every dark crevice that makes him who he is ... it only makes me want to love him more ... even if it gets me killed.

The phone ringing on the nightstand sends a jolt of panic through me. As if I've been caught in the act of thinking too much, thinking about things I shouldn't be.

I stare at it from where I am. Even though Declan gave it to me, it's not really my phone. Even as I answer the call I know, it's just another test.

"Mama," I say, greeting her with a tone that's meant to appease her.

"Nena, where are you?" Her words are riddled with so much emotion. "I'll come pick you up." The eagerness in her voice pains me.

"A little sick."

"Still?" I've always been a bad liar and I hate to lie to my mother. I'd be a fool to think Declan or his family at least, doesn't have this phone wired or tapped or whatever the hell they do. As I sit on the edge of the bed, I get a look at the money again. I don't trust anything. It's all a damn test and I just want it to be over so my life can go back to normal. Or as normal as it can ever be after all of this.

"I just want to stay in and watch shows, Mama."

"Let me bring you soup," she suggests, her voice hopeful. "It's been too long that you've been sick. Let me check on you."

"I'll see you soon, Mama, but I can't see you right now." There's a hesitation on her end. Silence is all I'm given and inside I'm filled with shame. So much so that tears prick the back of my eyes. How? I don't know. They're sore and red rimmed from days on end of sobbing. I've never felt so weak and helpless. So utterly fucking useless and pathetic.

"Are you angry with me?" my mother asks quietly and I have to gather my composure.

"No, no, Mama," I say as quickly as I can.

"Is this about Travis?" It's after she says his name that I can tell my mother is crying. It fucking kills me. I hate this. I hate all of it.

"No, Mama. Please. I just ..." I want to tell her a sliver of the truth. I fell in love with someone I shouldn't have. But instead I tell her, "I miss you, Mama, and love you. Don't worry. I'll see you soon."

"Why can't I see you now?" As my mother questions me, a low, steady beep comes from the window. It startles me at first; it seems like anything and everything does now. It takes a moment for me to realize it's a truck. They're doing construction outside like Declan told me they would. Aria's words come back to me; she said it would be the perfect time to run.

"I have to go, Mama," I tell her to try to get her off the phone before I say things I shouldn't.

"You would tell me if you were hurt or if someone was hurting you, wouldn't you?" She sniffles on the other end although with how muffled it is, it seems she's trying to hide it from me.

"Yes," I lie to her. "Of course I would."

"You're okay?" she asks again, as if she doesn't believe me and I wish she would. I wish she would be content with the lies.

"I'm just a little sick and I don't want to leave the bed." She carries on for a while, poking and prodding and I continue to lie to her. Over and over until she lets me hang up the phone. I'm not lying when I tell her I love her, though, and I hope I'm not lying when I say I'll see her soon.

My words stay with me even after the conversation is over: *I'm just a little sick and I don't want to leave the bed.*

When I hang up, I realize how true those words are. I don't want to leave the bed. I don't want to risk seeing his family. I don't want to risk walking down the corridor and remembering what happened in the room with the tub. I can barely breathe thinking about it now. As I lower myself to the mattress, I realize just how paralyzing this situation is.

All I want is to stay right here until Declan comes home and tells me what I can do. Because if I don't wait for him ... all I keep thinking is that I don't want to die.

Chapter 21

Declan

The relief I felt when I checked the security system and saw she didn't touch the money and she was still there in my bed waiting for me leaves me the moment I open the bedroom door and get a glimpse of the state she's in.

She didn't take the money. She didn't run. But my Braelynn is a shell of herself.

At the sound of the door closing, her wide, red-rimmed eyes peer up at me. Swallowing thickly, I push down the thought that resonates the most. Propped up on her side, her body's stiff as the silence settles between us. I fucking hate myself for what I've done to her.

"My mother called," she tells me as I unbutton the collar of my shirt. I can barely look at her as she tattles on herself.

"We talked briefly but I didn't tell her anything."

I hum a response and then pull my shirt over my head, letting it fall to the floor. As I kick my shoes off by their heels, I face her and a small smile forms on its own from the sight of her staring up at me.

Wanting approval, from me. She fucking needs it.

"You can talk to your mother whenever you'd like ... I trust you."

Her throat tightens as she swallows and then explains, "She wants to see me."

With one knee on the bed, I pause before giving her an inch of freedom. "If you want to see her, Nate can take you whenever and wherever you'd like."

I expect her to be relieved, maybe even excited but the blood drains from her face.

Under the baggy sweater, my Braelynn appears so small and fragile. Her lips are no longer the dark red that tempts me, her eyes carry that color instead. And it shames me.

"Nate?" She barely breathes his name. Fear takes residence in her expression. A crease settles in my forehead as my brow pinches. Is she so afraid she needs me to come with her? What did Aria tell her?

The bed groans as I lean back against the headboard and lay an arm out. "Come," I command gently.

I've never thought of Braelynn as frail or weak. Never once until this past week. I thought she simply needed to recover, but the woman who lies beside me, closing her eyes the moment her side meets mine — she's broken.

Her heart beats so fast and hard, I can hear it before she swallows thickly. "I don't want you out alone ..." I nearly tell her about the feds and the depositions. I nearly confess that there's a very strong chance she's going to be questioned about Scarlet's death. But peering down at her, she already appears on edge. Carter's words haunt me: she's fucking terrified.

"I wanted to go home and grab some things, swing by my mother's and if I—"

"Nate can take you or I can when a few things blow over."

Her deep brown eyes stay wide open, staring aimlessly at my chest.

I pull her closer and hold her tighter. I run my hand through her hair and attempt to comfort her.

"Could you take me tonight?" she questions and her voice is tight. As if she needs my answer to be yes.

McHale told me to stay in. Not to go anywhere. There's a high chance of a raid soon in The Club. How do I tell her that? "I'm stuck here too tonight, my naïve girl." Nate's deposition is scheduled, so there's no risk for him going out. She'll stay away from all the bullshit that being out with me puts her at risk of witnessing.

"You're stuck with me?" she questions in a raspy voice.

"It all needs to die down for the moment, so I'd rather we didn't go anywhere tonight or at all this week."

With a kiss on her temple, I expect her to understand but she doesn't.

"I can't stay here forever," she whispers.

"Whatever you need from your house, Nate can go get," I offer her.

She squirms uncomfortably. "I don't want Nate to take me anywhere or ..."

"Nate is going to look after you and do whatever I order him to do. You are mine," I tell her, gripping her chin and tilting it upward so she's forced to look at me. She averts her gaze until I run the pad of my thumb over her lips.

"He scares me," she confesses.

I almost ask her why, because I'm a fucking fool. She witnessed him murder her friend in cold blood. Even if she was a rat, it's something she's never seen. He was there in the room when everything happened to her ... when they tortured her.

I bring my lips lower, the tip of my nose brushing along hers and speak lowly and carefully so she hears every word. "Do you believe me when I tell you I would kill him if he ever made you feel uncomfortable?"

The thought enters my mind that it would ease so much of her worry if I simply let him go. If I slit his throat and he was eliminated from this complication. But everyone knows he has a deposition. The feds as well as my allies. It wouldn't be a good look in the least for me to kill three of my own men in a single week while cops are rounding up the others.

The web we've weaved is far too tangled.

"Yes," she answers and gives a short nod, her expression softening slightly. It doesn't ease my own irritation in the least.

"I told you, no one is going to hurt you."

"If that were true, though, I could leave ... unless this is a test. Unless I'm locked in here for some other reason," she tells me. Staring me in the eyes, as steady as can be.

"My sweet naïve girl, you say the quiet part out loud too often."

With that, I kiss her gently and as I do, she trembles in my embrace and I fucking hate myself all over again.

"Take your medicine," I tell her, wishing she could sleep through all of this.

Chapter 22

Braelynn

I could tell that he didn't want to leave me, and yet he did.

What does that say about him? What does it say about us?

At least he told me he wished he could tell me everything that's going on but he said it would be better if I didn't know.

I'm inclined to agree with that.

I've spent the last hour wondering if I simply waited in the foyer or the kitchen, if Aria would come. I bet they're all watching and waiting. The men would leave me alone to see what I'd do. But I don't want to be left alone. It would almost be better to be locked in here because then the thought of running wouldn't exist. I'd know I'm not able to.

The sound of construction outside wouldn't remind me that now is my only chance to run.

I've barely eaten anything. I simply haven't had an appetite. But given the state of my hunger, I have to. My stomach growls as I get out of bed, only to realize I'm still in the same clothes as yesterday. For a moment I consider changing, but I decide to just wash my face and brush my hair and teeth.

Even doing those simple tasks feels like a struggle and for a blip of a moment I'm reminded of what it was like when I was with Travis. When I fell into a horrible depression. As I spit out the water I rinsed my mouth out with, I stare at my reflection. A dull complexion and dark undereye circles stare back at me.

My first instinct is to call the doctor, but for what? I can't schedule an appointment. I'm fucking trapped here.

The *beep*, *beep*, *beep* of some construction vehicle backing up keeps me from breaking down entirely.

Gripping the edge of the sink, I remind myself, all I have to do is obey. It won't be like this forever. It's simply a test, isn't it?

As I walk out, I consider taking my phone. There are unread messages from my mother and there's no access to social media on it. I leave it there, and head down the quiet hall.

The doors that line it are still shut and I don't know what's behind them. I don't dare look. I don't dare do anything other than walk to the far end that leads to the foyer. There's no curiosity anymore. There is only waiting and the silence that's filled with unwanted thoughts.

I'll make coffee and maybe that will give me energy. I'll eat something and then wait in the kitchen. There's a large window there and the light will do me good. And maybe Aria will come. If she sees me, maybe she'll have some sympathy for me.

Maybe I won't be alone with my thoughts and memories that won't be quiet. My bare feet pad against the cold marble floor. As the *beep, beep, beep* gets louder, the irony of it all hits me.

In this place of luxury, I'm a pawn and a prisoner. All because I fell in love with a boy who I thought needed help. Who I wanted to help but didn't know how.

Maybe in some fucked-up way, I did this to myself. Light filters in through the massive front doors. They're gorgeous and intricate and I haven't attempted to open them even though Declan said he'd leave them unlocked. He even gave me the code: 71017.

Vaguely I wonder if he did. I think about waiting here for Aria and asking her to open them. Just to see. I only want to know if he lied to me. If that's the test.

I take a few steps closer, but not close enough to touch, only to look out just a bit. Only to see what I can see while I'm far enough away for him to know I won't run. There are cameras. They are always watching when I'm outside of the room. I know that much.

It could be over if only I asked her to open them. I wouldn't do it. I wouldn't dare.

As I stand there, wondering if it could really all be done with if only someone opened the doors, a man's voice that chills me to my core is heard from the other side of the doors.

Paralyzed, I stand there and his shadow is cast along the carved glass.

"So it's true, then? That bitch sent it?"

I can't breathe. Nate's voice brings me back to the freezing cold bath. Over the memory of my screams I hear him say, "Declan's going to lose his fucking mind. I don't want to be the one to tell him."

I try to inhale but my head is light and nothing inside is working right. My body trembles as I remember the bath.

"You're sure it was Braelynn?"

I nearly collapse right there at the mention of my name and the venom he holds behind his statements. I don't see another shadow and it takes me too long to realize he's on the phone and he's getting closer.

What did I do?

"All I know is, I don't want to be the one to do it this time."

My head spins as his heavy footstep approaches. *He's coming for me.*

I run, as quickly and silently as I can, throwing open the door and I don't stop. I nearly fall as I come up to the bedroom door and inside, panic ensues.

Every word he said plays back to me: *So it's true, then? That bitch sent it?*

"I didn't send anything," I murmur to myself as I pace at the end of the bed, staring at the bedroom door.

Sickness churns as I worry that Declan won't believe me.

I didn't do anything. I didn't, did I? If I did, I didn't mean to. I didn't know.

Heaving in air, I try to calm myself but I can't. Instead all I can hear is the cage dropping into the water and my screams.

I'm blinded by it all and I act without thinking.

Rushing to put clothes on top of the money in the bag, I've never acted so fast in my life. All the while tears stream down my face and the vision in front of me is Declan, as I'm lowered into the water and left there.

They'll never believe me. Even if he loves me, they'll never trust me. They'll never let me leave. I scribble a note I don't know is even legible. *I'm sorry.*

I'm out of breath and can barely see straight when I get to the foyer. It's silent when I open the door to Declan's wing. My heart races as I listen for Nate's voice.

No one's there and in a rush of adrenaline, I rush to the front doors and input the code. I hold my breath until they unlock and pull open so very easily. With the heavy door ajar, I'm met with a biting cold and a reminder I need to hurry.

Chapter 23

Declan

The Club once felt like my hunting ground. Safe, controlled and secured. I could do whatever I'd like and rule over every soul who entered this place.

But now as I rewind the footage once again, with my tired eyes focused on the screen filled with the image of Braelynn, it feels like a prison.

One of my own making.

There has to be something I missed. I only have an hour, maybe two before the feds will be here. Or so the tip said. I wanted it done here. Not with Braelynn watching.

They'll raid. I'll be present and be picked up for questioning. Shortly after, I'll be hit with a subpoena for a deposition. It's all been done before and I couldn't care less.

All I care about is what's on these fucking tapes. Whispers in the back of my mind warn me that it's all there.

There's a knock on the door a second after I hit play, and I call out for them to go away. "I'm not here. Leave."

I'm left with the sound of retreating footsteps and in the corner of my eye, the security cameras capture the bar nearly packed, the stage curtains closed but ready to open as the night descends. It's all patrons. There's no one I'm concerned about in this whole damn place right now.

There's no break in this life. No moment of reprieve. Even as I beg the footage to show me something, anything at all, I'm not given a moment for it all to just stop.

There were only so many hours she was left alone with the computer. I know from history she didn't email anything or save information to portable storage.

There were only a handful of details given to the feds. A few lines that she must've memorized. No one else touched that computer. In the security footage, she doesn't save data onto a USB. But she also doesn't take any notes. A note that someone else could find or a note she was paid to make.

There's no way around it. There was incriminating evidence in drug sales on the spreadsheets and she remembered them because they didn't make sense, fed the information to someone and that's the only possible explanation.

The numbers don't exist in reality. They're fake. Planted there just for her.

She taps away on the screen in the video, occasionally looking across the office to my empty chair. I swear she smiles in fondness and I have to rewind the footage.

I swear she loves me even here. It makes no sense.

How could she want me like she does here, while planning on turning over evidence? Frustration gets the best of me and I throw the fucking remote across the room, smashing it into the drywall. The damage is minimal and I couldn't care less.

I don't fucking know what happened, but I believe her.

There has to be a reason other than Braelynn handing over the information. She would have had to memorize it since she didn't leave the office with it. Exact numbers. It's not difficult, but it doesn't seem like Braelynn.

The video plays and I watch as the door opens and my Braelynn straightens her posture, peering up at me and waiting for an order. I watch as I grasp her chin, lower my hand to her throat and kiss her. No, I fucking devour her and she leans into my touch. Eager and wanting. The laptop falls to the floor and she doesn't stop it. She doesn't care about it.

My chest tightens with an uncomfortable ache.

I really fucking love her. I should marry her, just in case they pick her up. Then she can leave. She can go anywhere and the feds can't legally question her about me. No one would dare touch her if she had my ring on her finger. None of this would fucking matter.

I think she'd do it. If she could leave without worry, she'd agree to it in a heartbeat.

My brothers would leave us alone. They would learn to trust her when all of this blows over. And it will. I won't allow it to linger and taint her reputation or mine. They'll all see that she's good and good for me.

I watch as the screen plays nothing but an empty room after I lead her away. The laptop closed and the room quiet. Every minute of footage is like this. She's the only one who touched it and there's no explanation that makes sense. But I don't give a fuck about logic or reason anymore.

They'll learn to love her and she'll learn to love them and the ways of this life. Just as the thought hits me, my phone vibrates in my pocket and I pull it out to see Carter calling.

He'll give his blessing. I know he will. Even still, I'm anxious to answer the phone. I can't shake this feeling.

"Carter," I answer and clear my throat. I lean back in my seat but stiffen when I hear the tone in his voice.

"Declan, where are you?" He already knows what's happening today.

Chills prick down my arm. "At the bar waiting for the—" I answer.

"She left. Half the money and left you a note."

"No." The word leaves me even though even I can hear the denial that's wrapped around the single syllable.

"I'm sorry," he tells me, his tone full of remorse. Clicking over to the tabs for my room, I flick through them, each and every one.

My gaze flicks to the empty screen, willing her to be there, but she's not.

"Do you want me to read the note?" he asks and the blood drains from my face.

"What does it say?"

"I'm sorry. I love you. I can't stay here anymore. I swear, I didn't mean to."

"I wonder what they gave her. What the feds could have offered her that would make her want to work with them," I say.

"She was friends with Scarlet ... you know how those things go. It's possible Scarlet dragged her in ... maybe she didn't realize until it was too late." Carter offers an explanation but it doesn't do shit to keep me upright as the reality hits me.

"She could have told me. At any point, she could have—"

"She was scared, Declan. We all saw it."

"Well no shit, she sold us out." The anger is dull. There's nothing but fucking heartache that overwhelms me.

"She didn't call them. She called her mother and that's it."

"Her phone is still bugged?"

"Yeah."

"What did she tell her?"

"That she misses her but she's scared," he answers and the back of my throat dries and I have to clear it once again. I fucking hate this. With my hands going numb I run them down my face.

How the hell did this happen? I don't understand. I loved her. She loved me.

"You there?" my brother questions.

"What else?"

"That she's going away for a while and that she loves her."

"Do you have the recording?"

"Yeah. It sounded like she wasn't coming back, Declan. She tossed the phone and left the car ... took a taxi or hitched after that."

"We know where she is?"

"Yeah ... all that cash and she went to a shitty motel down the interstate."

Chapter 24

Braelynn

I can't stop stop crying. My chest heaves as I try to calm the sobs.

What have I done?

I've never been so terrified in my life. My entire being is heavy with guilt. I've never felt so reckless and like I can't go back, I can't make it better. I thought once that I'd been at the lowest low possible, but I knew nothing.

I betrayed a man I loved. A man who if I ever see again will certainly have me killed.

I don't even know who I am anymore or how any of this happened. I want to take it all back. Burying my hot face into the pillow does nothing but mute the sobs from creeping through the paper-thin walls of this shitty motel.

The mattress is cheap, the sheets stiff from too much starch and the comforter a holdover from the eighties. There's enough money in that bag to stay at hotels I've never imagined myself in, but I couldn't bring myself to face more people than needed. There's no lobby here, just a teller at a window where cash is slipped under the plexiglass divider and a key is given in return.

There's a chair that looks to be decades old, a laminate desk, a single bed and the kind of old-fashioned bulky TV I haven't seen in ages and didn't know existed anymore. From the single window beside the bed, the traffic from the highway blows into the room with a gust of wind. My face is hot and more than once I've looked outside, at the five-story distance to the asphalt below.

I've thought about leaving the money for my mother. But they'd find it and then her, I'm certain of it. Fresh tears prick hot and unrelenting. I hate them and I hate myself.

I wish I could call her and tell her everything, but I can't drag her into this. It would only be selfish. The old landline phone stares back at me, willing me to call her, but I won't.

I could go to the hospital, but he'd find me there. My mother might even find me there and then I wouldn't be able to protect her. I have to be alone or go back to Declan.

I picture myself begging him, on my knees and pleading with him rather than running.

Half of the time I imagine it, he tells me it's okay. The

other half he looks at me as he did in the basement of The Club, telling me I should be terrified.

With my hands clasped to prevent them from shaking, I do everything I can to just calm down. I brush my teeth and change into a nightgown as though I'm going to bed. I wish I had the meds Declan's been giving me to stop it all. To put me to sleep where I can't think about anything at all. I would do anything and take anything not to think right now, to just go to sleep and make it stop.

It's like even though I've left, I'm still trapped.

I'll never feel safe. I don't know what to do.

I wish I could erase all of this. But all of the wishes don't mean shit, do they? I fucked up ... again. Every thought I have is that there's only one way to end it. The horns and screech of tires from down below drift into the room. A drizzle of rain starts and it's almost comforting. It would at least be over, then.

No more terrifying memories of Scarlet's eyes wide with fear before Nate snapped her neck.

No more of the cage being lowered into the tub.

No more of second-guessing my every move for fear of disappointing Declan.

I don't know what happens once you die, but it can't be worse than this. Than every regret stealing your breath and every fear paralyzing you.

I don't think there was ever a real chance for us. I was

never going to be good enough and he warned me. To his credit, he warned me. I wish he never wanted me and I could have just loved him from afar.

The memory of our first kiss plays back in my head. When he gripped my wrists and pinned me there. When kissed me like I was his and had always been his. The warmth, the way everything else faded.

At least I know what it was like to kiss Declan Cross.

And I swear I did feel loved by him. Even if it was just for a moment. Even if love wasn't enough.

Just as I open my eyes, letting the memory go, there's a gentle click at the flat wood door. I'm still as the knob turns and the door creaks in an eerie way.

I don't bother to move. I only watch as if it's a movie. I'm numb to it all until he stands there in the open threshold.

"Declan." I whisper his name as the sight of him registers.

Sniffling, I sit up straighter, pulling the sheet closer. *Is this real?*

"There you are ... you thought I'd let you go?"

It's crazy, the smile that wants to pull at my lips as I sniffle. The warmth from knowing at least he wouldn't let me run. He wouldn't let this torture last too long. It's absolutely fucking insane that I'm grateful I won't have to end it myself.

Tears leak from the corner of my eyes and I wipe them away as I manage to say, "I thought you might find me."

"You didn't run far," he says lowly, closing the door behind him and looking back only to lock it.

My movements are rigid and slow as I pull my knees into my chest. I can't look away from him, from the look of betrayal in his sharp steely gaze, or the anger that radiates from his broad shoulders as he stalks toward the bed. The floor groans with every step and all I can do is wait for him.

I wasn't prepared for this life—I had no idea what loving a man like Declan would be like. The intensity and how hard and fast I would fall, but how I would step on every land mine not realizing I needed to just stay still. I wish I could go back. In another life, we are meant for each other, but in this one, I'm not good enough. I wasn't prepared and in his world, one mistake could end your life. I've made more than my fair share of mistakes.

As he sits on the edge of the bed, I can picture his hand wrapping around my throat and I have to at least apologize first. I don't think he'll believe him if I were to tell him I love him, but he has to know I'm sorry. Fuck, I'm so pathetic it's obvious that I'm sorry.

"I'm sorry," I whisper and the words are choked, barely audible.

Roughly, I wipe the pathetic tears away. My hands tremble as I do and to my surprise, Declan holds me.

He doesn't shush me, but he brings me into his chest and the moment he shows me that bit of compassion, I break beneath him, clinging to him and holding onto him when I know I have no right.

With my head buried into his chest, I close my eyes and fall apart.

His hand runs up and down my back as he lays us down, silently but gently.

He allows me the moment to grieve and I wish I could stop it. I wish I wasn't the pathetic regretful mess I am, but I can't stop it. By the time I'm done, both my body and eyes are heavy. It's like everything has given up. Sleep could pull me in now and take me forever.

My eyes open and I stare at the button on his collar. Inhaling his masculine scent and enveloped by his warmth, I dare to whisper into his chest, "Can you do it in my sleep?" My heart beats once, a dull thud. He's still, unresponsive, and I know I'm every bit the coward when I beg him, "I know I don't deserve it, but if you could," I pause to take in a shuddered breath before continuing, "if I could be asleep, I think it could be peaceful."

I'm left with shock and uncertainty as he swiftly pulls away and leaves me alone on the bed, slamming the bathroom door behind him.

CHAPTER 25

DECLAN

I must be fucked in the head, but then again, I always have been. The back of my eyes sting as I grip the edge of the cheap pedestal sink in this shithole. The mirror is cracked and the silvering peeling off in one corner and my vision moves from it to my reflection as I do everything I can to just breathe.

Everything fucking hurts. Every piece of me is sickened and numbed from years of this fucked-up life.

She wants me to kill her while she sleeps. While she holds on to me, and falls asleep in my arms, she thinks I could do such a thing. I fucking love her. I love her more than I ever thought I could.

All I see when I look at Braelynn is someone I want to protect. Someone I would burn the world to the ground for.

How can she not see that? Am I truly such a monster she'd rather die? My hand shakes as I reach for my phone while it buzzes in my back pocket.

All she had to do, was stay with me ... but I should have known better. She is sweet and naïve, she's curious and reckless ... but how could a woman like her ever want to stay with me?

The screen lights up the bathroom as a storm brews outside. The small paned window in the cramped bathroom is cracked and a brisk breeze blows in. My entire body feels as if it's on fire one minute, then chilled the next.

Are you with her? Carter texts and my throat closes.

I've never felt such shame. My shoulders heave forward and it takes every ounce of control in me not so smash my fist into the mirror, shattering the glass.

This pain is something I've never felt. With my eyes closed and my breathing coming in ragged I try to hold it all back. To shove it all down.

I don't want any of this to be real anymore. I just want to go back. To rewind it all.

If ever there was a God who would listen to my pleas, I beg him now, please stop this. Hell, I'd sell my soul to the devil himself to make it stop. To make her happy and safe. Even if it means a life without me.

I'd rather die than for her to think I'd ever hurt her.

Crash! Bang! "Hands where we can see them!" Shock rips

through me at the sound of the door to this shit motel room being kicked in. It's nearly surreal as I walk out, the bathroom door creaking open in complete opposition to the screaming and chaos.

"Freeze!"

"Get on the floor, get on the floor!"

"Declan Cross, come out with your hands up!"

"Hands behind your back!" The moment they see me, orders are made. My response is nearly automatic. I've been arrested more times than I can count, let alone remember.

"On what grounds?" My tone is flat as I focus on Braelynn, still under the covers, her eyes wide with new fear.

"It's okay," I try to tell her but an officer speaks over me. I don't recognize any of these men. All decked out in tactical gear, there are six of them to just the two of us. A chill runs down my spine.

"You're wanted in the questioning of Scarlet Miller's murder." The blood drains from my face at the mention of her name. But I've been through this shit before. This is a game I can play. "Don't say anything, Braelynn. Don't consent to a search. Don't talk to anyone other than to tell them you want your lawyer."

Deep voices cry out and guns are held by men in uniform, pointing not just at me, but at Braelynn. Anger tears through the denial, through the shame. Through fucking everything.

"Leave her alone!" With both hands in the air, I scream

to Braelynn that it's okay. Her hair is disheveled, her eyes red rimmed. My heart only beats again when she looks at me. It beats as if it's the last time blood will flow through my veins. It all happens too fast once I register what she's going to do. I can't stop it.

"I'm sorry," she whispers before ignoring their warnings and running to the window. She's reckless, my naïve girl. *No, no, don't jump. Please, save her.* My motions aren't fast enough, and I can't rip my arms from their grasp.

"Braelynn, no!"

About the Author

Thank you so much for reading my romances. I'm just a stay at home Mom and an avid reader turned Author and I couldn't be happier.

I hope you love my books as much as I do!

More by Willow Winters
www.willowwinterswrites.com/books

This is the Discreet Edition so no-one knows what you are reading.

You can find each edition at

www.willowwinterswrites.com/books

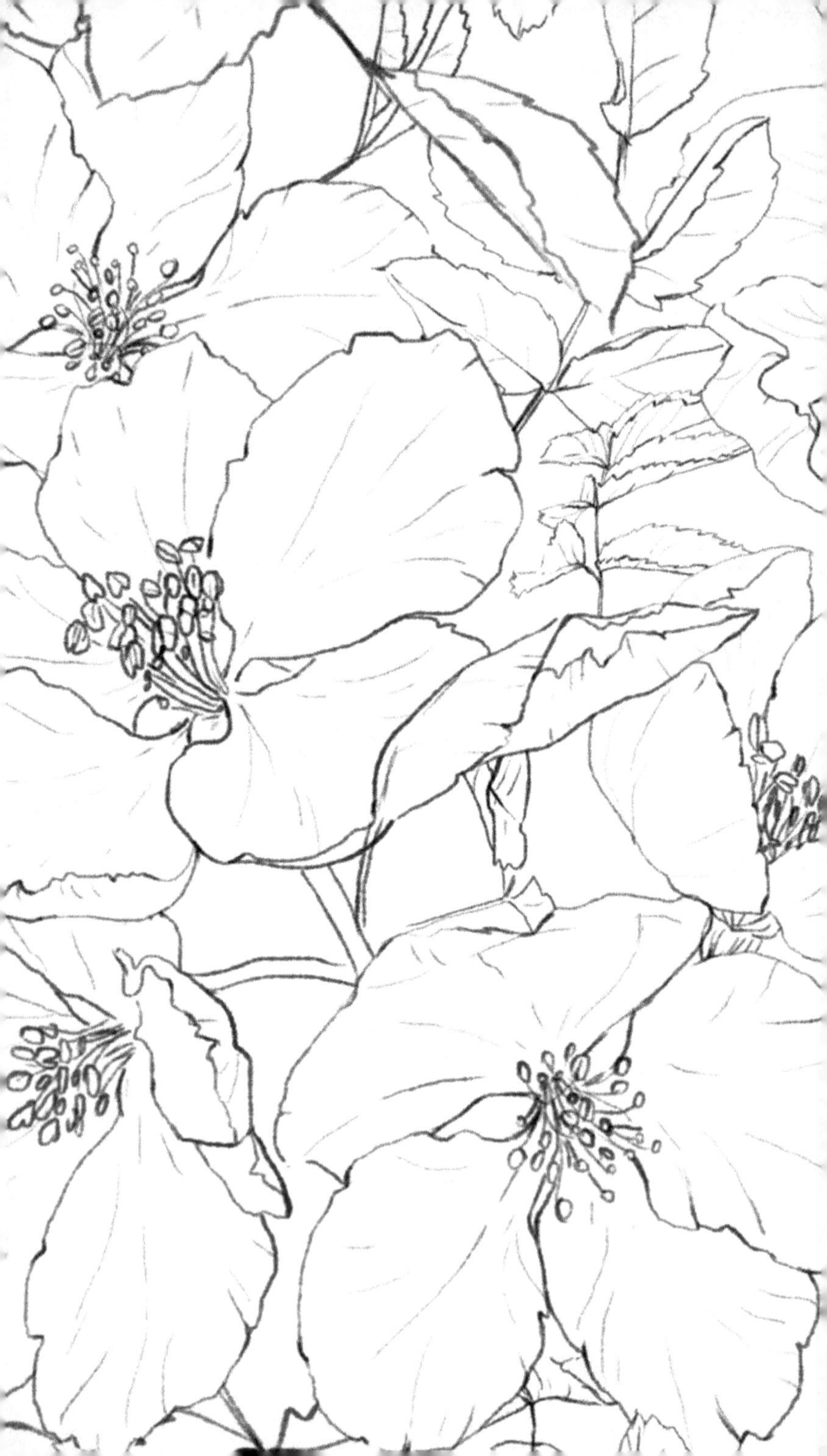

Printed in the USA
CPSIA information can be obtained
at www.ICGtesting.com
JSHW082247240124
55713JS00004B/15